Trial By Robot:
A Spiritual Allegory For
Modern Times

Other works by this author can be found @gotwords.org

Trial By Robot:
A Spiritual Allegory For Modern Times

LA Jamison

Contributors Dan Miron, Don Naggy, Angela Carter, & Chris Hajjar

GOTWORDS? Publishing

2018

First Printing: 2018

ISBN 978-0-9861549-4-2

GotWords? Publishing 14609 Jonas Ave.
Allen Park, MI 48101

www.gotwords.org

Dedication

To my two favorite Anthonys: Anthony Cecchini and
Anthony Gosur, for all your unconditional support and love.

Contents

Acknowledgements

I would like to thank my special contributors made by Dan Miron, Donald Naggie, Angela Carter, and Chris Hajjar. Many thanks!! This book wouldn't be the same without your contributions!

Preface

Preface: Roots of the Trial of the Future

The idea for this novella dropped upon my brain like a raindrop. I was walking on a track at my local recreation center with this rather vague wish for the world to have a better spiritual experience, and then it was as if the universe just handed this story over to me. I felt it was not only an exciting idea to write, but my duty to write it. In reflecting back to the sub-layers of motivation behind this story, I identified three central ideas. First, I desired to write a multi-layered story similar to some of the classics such as many Hawthorne's short stories like The Birthmark, Rappaccini's Daughter and the Scarlet Letter. This would take a variety of hidden gems in the form of symbols and allusions of which I chose to use not only in a spiritual sense, but also in homage to other sci-fi/fantasy stories and films. Second, I wanted this story to appeal to that part of us which would put our own creator(s) on trial and kill him/or her for failing us, the created. A rather ballsy idea, if I may use that crude term. Finally, I wanted a story that explored this notion that many people use to dismiss the spiritual and supernatural. That is, the willingness to put human ideas around logic on such a pedestal that it should always overrule the senses and those things that are unexplained. I find it fascinating that so much of the supernatural is dismissed because a certain group of people won't wrap their mind around what they can't physically taste, see, touch and smell. Of course, I'm not "for" the totally illogical beyond the entertainment value, but I think we as humans are way too limited to not keep an open mind and heart about that which may be beyond our human limited scope.

It wasn't until I was in college and took my first literature class that the classics took on life for me. My very first literature professor was able to bring out the rich symbolism, metaphors and allusions that many of these stories hold and are still speculated over unto this day. Theories of a deep revealing nature that can connect to a reader's life today through stories set in all the way back to 1800's is something remarkable to me. These kind of stories are time machines. It not only gives one a lot of excitement and individual reflection, but it also provides for rich discussion in small groups. To this end, I created this companion to facilitate both individual and group reflections. This is located in the back of the book.

Though there is a focus on Christian symbolism woven throughout the story, it is a story reflecting the struggle with the idea of spirit that is common in all religions. The Christian spiritual references are tools of a purely spiritual and historical nature and not meant to proselytize anyone into a Christian belief system. You will not find a hidden agenda of getting readers through "the steps to salvation". What I do use this particular faith for is only toward those common elements of human life and spirituality we have questions about and that I find are worthwhile to explore. I suppose that is my writer's privilege to explore them. Christianity, when used in this story and in group discussion questions, is as a springboard to such discussions that anyone should be able relate to. And though the Bible can be an highly debatable book and for others a faulty book of cruelty and contradictions, I find that even if that was the case, this is still a book of literature and an ancient one at that. It is worth talking about for that merit alone--though I personally find other merits as well.

The spiritual elements I weave throughout the story are set against the background of pure, resounding logic. In this case, humanoids are programmed to value logic over everything else. This brings to focus the essential question of the novella, "Are there any values at all to a spiritual life, and what would those values be?"--even for those who deny its value because of logic. Since we often have constructs in our mind about our everyday lives, it is hard for us to be open to new ideas in stories that are similar to our own daily lives. "I've heard it all before" and "Been there, done that" kind of mind frames can hinder readers from hearing ideas they may have overlooked in very creative stories. It is much easier for us to read into such text and media from our perspective when they are set in backgrounds like our own. We tend to go where we find comfort. And for many, it can be like scaling a thousand foot wall to get beyond their own beliefs and experiences. By casting this story in the future, we can disarm our own preconceived notions about not only the "now" but the future. We can be open to new ideas because we are vulnerable again within a world we aren't familiar with or know how to navigate.

Lastly, in our day and age, whether it is religion or politics, we are wrestling with a lot of extremism, which threatens our societies with ideas that would take people backwards rather than forwards. While branded with the loftiest ideas around life and patriotism, these extremist ideologies march before weary minded people. They empower people who feel ostracized because of their own internal hatred and who long for a platform to defend their hatred rather than being educated through compassion. We all want to be heard. No matter who you are, you want to have a platform. However, hate and beliefs developed from it don't deserve a public platform beyond public scrutiny. They certainly should not be a part of our laws. "Trial By Robot" explores this struggle with a religious sect called the Descendants and the trial itself as a cruel exploration that is both political and humanitarian in nature.

I'm excited to think people would use this companion in addition to the story itself to explore the richness of what on the surface could appear as a very simple text, just as I did in those literature classes years ago. Enjoy the read!

I.

Vincent was sped along one of Acropolis' superhighways in a black aircraft shaped in the form of a giant bullet. Hands folded as though he were praying and looking out the passenger window from the backseat, Vincent's ocean blue eyes blinked like two puddles in a soft rain. He brought his palms down to his thighs and watched the city buildings blur together into a psychedelic rainbow as the vehicle flew across the air highway. The lights from other flying vehicles streaked across the night's dark canvas. Something about the case he would interpret seemed special. Even the colors before his eyes seemed brighter. The city beckoned him to exact just judgment in accordance to the law of humanoid kind.

Vincent gave a small frown as he looked at the bar code on the top of his right hand- #G220. It identified his model number to the scanners throughout the quadrant. He never liked this mark that interrupted the perfection of his skin but it was a necessary sacrifice to distinguish humanoid from human. This was without question. The humanoid took a glance at himself in the driver's side rear view mirror. He stroked his feathered hair which the droid kept light brown for the season. He could change style and color by a simple wink to an internal program, and he debated briefly whether a darker color might be suitable for the courts. However, he thought the better of it. He became suddenly unsure about his nose. For the first time, he noticed that it appeared unusually large. He wasn't happy with it. So, with a few internal winks to certain software programs, he changed his nose size in a matter of seconds. Done.

He adjusted his suit jacket letting out a sigh. He hated how contract jobs at the Chancery made him second guess himself. Small changes like this were permissible while larger facial reconstructions required permission from the courts. They were also much more taxing on his system--in some cases causing temporary blindness.

Vincent's government-provided vehicle drove itself to the intended destination--The Grand Inquisitor. Acropolis' city buildings went from tall, spiked architecture to smaller rounded buildings as they reached the downtown area. It was theorized that these taller outer buildings acted as a shield to the government buildings nestled deep in the center of Acropolis. It was a magnificent display of metallic colors and creative architecture beyond compare anywhere else in the quadrants. The tall humanoid whose head was only about one inch from the car ceiling leaned forward as the vehicle approached the towering Grand Inquisitor. It was a tightly secured lodging facility--reserved for high level government employees. It stood as a black monolith looming over the Supreme Chancery.

As the Chancery was wide and long in scope, the Inquisitor was in height. Vincent's black chariot, assigned VIP status, penetrated a dark opening just before one of several grand staircases and flew down the tunnel into the parking garage.

The black capsule speedily docked itself to the nearest platform under ground level. Vincent was never connected to the importance of his role as Court Report Interpreter

13

more than he was with this most noteworthy case. Trials took place for humanoid disobedience or debates over the fine nuances of the law in an ever-changing world; however, the Chancery was by and large put in place for the trial of humans and human sympathizers. The law and the display of enacting justice was something most humanoids cherished. Even if some of the older laws were mocked and found passé to updated models, most foundational laws could not be erased. All humanoids loved discussing the fine nuances of the law to show who knew the law best. This particular trial would be one for the record books because of the intricacies of the defendant being both humanoid and human. As Vincent thought about this, he wrapped the palm of his right hand around his neck for a moment.

Vincent was somewhat embarrassed by the onset of recurring tension in his neck that was more frequent as of late. It could get where it seemed almost impossible to turn his head. This onset of tension was episodic in nature and felt like his neck muscles had grown stiff with age and undo- stress. In addition, he could feel the fluid exchange fibers pulsating in his neck whenever the episodes came on. This was a reaction in his system he did not understand. It wasn't a reaction that he had heard of other humanoids experiencing, and so he refused to have it checked out. Instead, he kept it a secret and did his best to cope with the symptoms.

Any form of stress on their systems was supposed to be cared for by stress regulators that were superior to adrenal glands in humans. By and large, humanoids did not feel-- not that they did not have the capacity for some low level emotion but nothing terribly noticeable. Anything more would be considered a sign of weakness. However, there were rumors that the humanoid race had evolved in their ability to feel and emote much more than say a hundred years ago. Systems within humanoids were creating their own systems. To what extent they were undergoing such an evolution was impossible to know but this development was both exciting and frightening all at the same time.

The government of Acropolis kept such issues under a shroud of darkness and fog. The debate itself was something reserved for the elite and those far away from the all-seeing-eye of Acropolis. Vincent supported the government's role of slapping down the hands that reached for the chalice of ideas about any human-like evolution. After all, history proved where this kind of thing could lead. The unnecessary exaltation of humans resulted in the creation of underground labs. These labs which had been created by those who worshiped humans and chose to breed human fetuses with humanoid technology. An abhorrent fantasy that if anything ever made the humanoid experience any level of nausea, this vision came the closest.

These human sympathizers also had worked with the corpses of adult sized humans conducting freakish experiments in an attempt to give humanoids human parts. How could anyone worship a species that had nearly destroyed the planet? Human systems were remarkably complex but fragile, and their egos and emotions over-ruled the better part of themselves, destroying everything good in their path. No, it was best that humanity be eliminated and not somehow made into a hybrid race with humanoid parts. They would only one day bring the Earth to edge of destruction once again. In Vincent's mind, it was an insult to humanoid-kind.

Upon exiting the vehicle, Vincent noted a download dumped in his data bank that had come off a government news channel. The file was entitled "Is this the end of the Galatian stand-off?". He slowed his stride on the metal docking bay and opened the file. After the file opened, Vincent's vision was penetrated with the vision of a humanoid news anchorwoman streaming through his retina so that her image appeared to be floating before him like an apparition. There was a smaller image near her head of a man in mechanized locks around his wrists and ankles. He was no ordinary man. Indeed, he wasn't even an ordinary prisoner. This was the governor of one of the last remaining outposts of human congregates, Governor John Woods. He was from the frozen area known as Galatia, one of the last remaining hybrids (if not the last), and Vincent was assigned to his case.

What he knew of Governor John Woods was more than most. Vincent had served in the military years prior and this gave him certain connections not all Court Report Interpreters had. Woods was a controversial leader over one of the last remaining tribes of humans in the Arctic territory of Galatia. There was no known hybrid who had risen to such ranks among humans. This in itself was an amazing feat. The Galatians lived under almost constant blizzard like conditions. This made operations nearly impossible for the military of Acropolis. The humans were deeply entrenched there and had decades of survival skills that gave them the advantage over Acropolis' military force.

Governor Woods was now not only one of the last remaining pillars of strong leadership for human resistance in the North, but he was also last of a hybrid race. He stood as the last living betrayal toward humanoid-kind, and now he was here, in Acropolis.

Vincent made his way off the departure docking station and checked in at the Express Reservation Desk manned by an older model droid. The Reservation droid was redone with gold plating and shined brilliantly among the colors of maroon floor and black walls. It moved behind its small desk with quick, exact movements, handling the line up of many government clients and envoys as though it were on an assembly line. It showed no confusion or fatigue.

After check-in, Vincent entered an elevation tube where, business suit and all, he was jettisoned with a burst of air upward to the floor of his room. He didn't enjoy the feeling of the suction pulling on his skin but always appreciated speed and efficiency. The humanoid walked out of the tube on floor 40, readjusted his suit jacket and grip on his briefcase and walked toward his room. He walked down the hallway carpeted in the same colors as all government buildings--orange, maroon, and pale yellow. The entire floor, stretching out longer than his eyes could see, was eerily quiet; so much so that he could hear the brushing of his gray suit pants and jacket against his body. It tickled the sensors in his ears.

Vincent entered room 71a, and stood stationary within the dark as if to digest some sense of its undisturbed nature. He took this pause before what would no doubt be intense proceedings that could last days.

"Lights, low level," Vincent said watching the lights come on as softly as he had spoken the request.

"Welcome Vincent. It is good to have you back in the city again," said a throaty voice in the room.

"Thank you, Ava, it has been some time."

"Thank you for your service to the Republic today," the woman's voice said as if reuniting with a long-lost friend, "I hope your time at the reservation desk was satisfactory?"

"As always, Ava," Vincent said non-enthusiastically and placed the briefcase on the low standing dresser.

The tall, lean humanoid dressed in all black walked over to the far opposite end of the room. He waved his hand over a small scanning mechanism that sat on an end table with a Tiffany style lamp. It's multicolored, holographic shade subtly changed colors like a kaleidoscope on slow motion. When the scanner recognized his hand pattern, part of a wall folded itself up like a tiled jigsaw puzzle and formed into a frame making a large window. The window revealed the grand architecture of the city on the horizon. Vincent approached the window and stood still with hands on hips. It felt as though he lived two lives whenever he took in the view of downtown Acropolis. The sea of tall, glassy visages climbing up to the sky circling the outer boundaries of the downtown sent rays of lights bouncing off their walls-- reflections bouncing off of reflections. This was far different from the rural quadrants of which he also traveled to in order to conduct investigations of human sympathizers.

Directly below was the unavoidable view of The Supreme Chancery. The Chancery wasn't tall as it was wide in its circular outreach that was rumored to cover two miles and maybe a little extra. A round garden courtyard was carved out in the center turning the rooftops and the surrounding trees it into a playground for birds whom knew nothing of the serious happenings going on inside it's walls. Its semi-circular design represented the world in which the Chancery tribunals judged. Vehicles of different sizes and shapes flew in traffic lines between the surrounding buildings like a line of bees. The uniformity of it all tickled his sensors. The humanoid shook his head and re-calibrated his focus to this historic trial. Court Report Interpreters not only oversaw the details of the transcripts but reported on the non-verbal cues during testimony. Unlike barbaric human courts, humanoids knew that non-verbal clues told more than verbal testimony and this was a Court Report Interpreters primary focus. The Supreme Chancellor made the final decision when the interpreters' decisions did not match the court tribunal. 98% of the time, the Supreme Chancellor went with the court interpreter's decision in such a case. In this sense, court interpreters were almost as important as the tribunal itself but without the same notoriety.

So begins the trial of the century, Vincent thought to himself. "No pressure though," he mumbled a loud.

"Pardon, Vincent, did you ask me something?" Ava asked.

"Oh no, I was merely talking to myself."

"Are you experiencing symptoms of stress?"

"Not at all, and I don't believe that's entirely possible."

"Talking to oneself is typically a response to stress, and though emotional stress is highly unlikely for your kind, there are other forms of stress. This is why you have secondary stress regulators.., and they are operating at slightly higher elevated levels compared to your prior stays with us. Can I do anything to make your stay more comfortable, Vincent?"

"No, I'm fine, really. Maybe it was the long journey here. I've been traveling a lot with back-to-back cases in many quadrants.

"Would you like me to get you some calming fluids? We have a variety of special teas and such-"

Vincent smirked, "That's not necessary, Ava." The humanoid gracefully walked over to his briefcase and sat on the edge of bed opening it as if it contained a priceless treasure. The humanoid pulled out an 8x11 sheet of glass and pinched the corner frame. It lit up and illuminated a picture of Governor John Woods in military uniform. Woods wore the typical, drab human cameo for human soldiers.

Vincent scrolled to another picture. This one was one of a woman on bent knee with her arms around two children. They seemed blissfully happy in their ignorance. He moved his fingers over to a video blast that revealed video clips with John's family, some with the Governor and some not. Vincent was reminded how, without the bar code identifier, that he resembled any other humanoid. He looked kind and intelligent enough on the outside. Yet, the reality was John Woods was a hybrid.

If there was one thing humans and humanoids shared, it was a distaste for hybrids. It was a sick irony that any humanoid would worship a human let alone being a part of a movement of creating hybrids. It was a horror that made no sense to the superior logic that ruled Vincent's thoughts. Humans themselves were low level, fleshy computers, but programmable nonetheless.., and still why? Why commune oneself forever to such problematic programming as human systems? These horrific experiments produced some truly horrid aberrations and miscarriages.

Even so, the human worshiper's technology soon had a short spell of successful hybrid reproduction. The underground labs themselves had been constructed where Acropolis never imagined looking for a betrayal of this magnitude--right under their nose in the downtown area. Acropolis was caught with their pants down. Nevertheless, once this minority of hybrids became large enough to be noticeable a threat, this movement was uprooted and secret labs were demolished. Hybrids were hunted down with a fierceness like never seen before. Ironically, exterminating humans themselves was not such an easy matter unless they were captured in battle. This was due to the older, what some termed more "pesky", foundational laws which were indisputable. They required fair trials for humans outside of committing acts of violence or espionage. Security protocols around some of these foundational laws--crafted during a time when humanoids were more sympathetic to humans--were virtually impossible to erase. The founders were sure to make it so.

Since erasing humans at will wasn't doable at this point, the Supreme Chancery had now turned these trials into a form entertainment, a mockery of a law they had to abide by, even in the light of human fallacy. Vincent played along with the showmanship but privately saw a courtroom as above such mockery, even if well deserved. It was yet another secret he held so close to himself. He saw the Chancery as a temple of their laws, which protected and guided the entire world. He longed for the day when the courts were once again more about their own development as a race than focused on the mockery of the weak, fragile human race. Once the human contingent, and their sympathizers were eliminated, Vincent hoped peace would reign in Acropolis and places like the Chancery would stand as a monument to their own superiority.

The humans would eliminate themselves,   Vincent reasoned.

Next, Vincent came across images of the governor's children. They were often seen in these clips expressing total glee, laughing and rolling around, even causing the surrounding adults to join in. Their innocent play exposed that they were clueless to the war about them. The woman, Woods wife, was quite beautiful in bone structure with high cheekbones, a well-rounded chin and unobtrusive nasal features. Her eyes were as blue as the sky, and she generally seemed to sincerely care about her family in the pictures and in the video clips with her children. This was clear by her physical gestures and facial expressions. He wondered where this joy and happiness came from when they were on the wrong side of the war and living in such poor conditions in arctic Galatia?

Vincent sighed and scrolled through more pictures and came across their snow covered military compound. Then, after that came the pictures of the men who had organized the mutiny. They appeared disheveled, wore long hair and beards--a gruff look Vincent was used to seeing from humans. Humans had a hard time trusting hybrids and so these five had ultimately turned their hybrid leader over to the Supreme Chancery--a real first in the history of the war! This development generated not only a lot of public interest in the trial but a most unusual result: an alliance. This band of five mutinous humans who had turned the Governor into the courts would testify on the side of the prosecution! The Governor was doomed!

This was a bold but ignorant move by the Galatian contingent who clearly saw this as some in-road to a truce with the Acropolis. Perhaps also making an example of him to their own people? The rumor was that these five mutineers may soon act as special envoys for some kind of humanoid/human relations "in order to keep the peace". Of course, if the desperate humans actually believed they would enter any type of partnership of peace, they would be bigger fools than they already had made themselves out to be. The city of Acropolis would never give human beings such a role when they were only a few crushing blows away from crushing them out completely. Nevertheless, humans were often fools, easily swayed by hope, and other inflated notions of thought generated by their primitive emotions. Fools, Vincent concluded.

Two additional pictures were that of one unusual looking humanoid who would be testifying. He was part of a religious sect of human sympathizers. He wore white priestly garb and a tall, gray cane which curved into a hook at the end. Vincent imagined the cane could be better used wrangling in some sheep or wild animals. He had heard of this radical religious group of human worshipers before, They called them themselves the Descendants. The Descendants abided by a strict code of service and conduct, and they worshiped a book written by a set of humans who they speculated to be creators of all humanoids. A purely, laughable notion; as if you humans could ever be so intelligent.

The Descendants called their organizing body "The Hewlett Packard" after the title on the book they worshiped. Thus, their full name being The Descendants of Hewlett Packard. It was no doubt to the advantage of the Galatians to take in these human sympathizers, humanoids or not, because they were desperate for numbers.

The Descendants of Hewlett Packard could be a very violent group when they felt they were extracting vengeance in light of any intolerance toward the first Descendants, which they insisted were human beings.

"Vincent, pardon me, but may I interrupt?"

"Yes, Ava, what is it?"

"You have an envoy from the Chancery in the lobby making their way up to your room. I wanted to make you aware of their arrival."

"The Chancery? Already? That's a little out of the ordinary... Very well." Vincent put the case file back in his briefcase and carefully set it back on the dresser. He let out a blast of air through his nostrils and sat on the bed with his hands placed delicately on each thigh and waited patiently. This was very unusual timing and not according to procedure which was almost as disturbing to him as a violation of law.

One of Vincent's forefingers began tapping his knee as the silence and anticipation gave him a feeling of tightness in his throat. Envoys from the Chancery were typically intimidating: Two men or two women from the same models with same builds. Twins. They often worked with the same mind, even finishing each other's sentences.

He was relieved momentarily to see two female envoys enter the room rather than the two towering men he had in a prior case. He stood up to greet the envoys and as usual they didn't respond but scanned the room as if eager to find violations. They wore the same colors but in opposing fashion; one wearing black pants and a white top and the other wearing white pants and a black top. One wore white lipstick, and the other black and same with the nail polish covering their unusually long nails. He noticed at once that they were taller than him with sharp features and piercing dark eyes. The one wearing the black lipstick called herself Cassandra and the one wearing white lipstick, Dee-Dee

"Not very charming," Vincent thought to himself. His belly quivered momentarily when one approached him, a sensation he hadn't felt in years. For an instant, he imagined this must be how those who had testified before the court must have felt being scanned and analyzed. Perhaps, Ava was right. Perhaps he was experiencing some form of stress more than he realized.

He noticed the other woman furthest away carrying a large briefcase that she sat down by the dresser while the other immediately went to his own smaller briefcase and emptied it out without asking. It was part of their job to examine everything. There were to be no secrets.

The other envoy examined his body language while asking the standard, routine questions. *Are you secure? Is the case file safe? Have you read the file thoroughly?* Blah, blah, blah. It was all the same routine data bytes from every envoy he ever encountered. At times, at night, he reorganized such routine conversations into music out of sheer boredom. Then something out of the ordinary happened. She circled him like a vulture might its prey, stood in front of him and ran a finger down the side of his cheek to his chin and kept it there. Was he picking up on the tension crushing his neck, he wondered as she examined him with a intensity he wasn't used to. She pucker lips which swiftly transitioned into a condescending smile.

"You have a question, a concern" Cassandra stated, "Ask it."

Dee-Dee chimed in, "I sensed that too Cassandra! Do tell us, Vincent, what is it?"

"Um... I-uh, not really a concern, per say... it is highly unusual to have an envoy from the Chancery here already. I just arrived, and surely the case isn't over already." Vincent smiled and then cleared his throat. The two women exchanged agreeing glances.

"The trial is over, Vincent. It has been going on in secret for days out of the public eye. We brought the trial files over for you to review via the Chancellor's command."

Vincent raised his eyebrows, "The trial is over? Are we speaking of the same trial? Of Governor John Woods?" The women looked on, unmoved and silent. "How? What about the backlash from the public!?! Trials of such high profile leaders are entertainment, the motivation to keep the public supportive of the war, is it not? This is a strange violation of procedure!"

Cassandra interjected, "The war is almost over. There will be more trials, I'm sure."

"One with the last remaining hybrid?"

"Oh, we doubt he represents the last. Once the public sees the guilty verdict, they will be energized to see the leader of Galatia fall. The government will give the public the highlights. That should satiate their appetite."

Dee-Dee came away from the dresser and chimed in from the distance, "The governing body of the tribunal has the final say so in such matters." They both then said in unison, "You of all citizens should know this."

Vincent brushed his cheekbone, "This is all very out of the ordinary...I suppose you are right to a degree. Who am I to question the Chancery? How long has the trial gone on?"

Cassandra cracked a smile as though he had said the right cue word. She came closer to him and handed him a computer chip the size of a large crumb. Vincent let it rest in his open palm and she softly closed his hands around it.

"Three days of record," she replied. Dee-Dee stepped forward snuggling up to her twin like a cat and placed herself arm in arm. "The Supreme Chancellor expects the report with the guilty verdict no later than tomorrow evening."

Vincent looked up from his cupped hand sensing some surprise which triggered the tension in his neck so much that he thought his neck might snap. He tried to subtly stretch his next as he pressed his lips together, took in a breath through his nostrils, and exhaled before speaking again. The envoys broke their entanglement and slowly turned away toward the door in attempt to let the humanoid get himself in check.

"I don't take pre-determined verdicts," Vincent insisted, "and how do you propose that I'm to report on three days of trials in 24hrs? This is an impossible request!" Vincent exclaimed.

Vincent, unsure what to do with his arms, folded his arms across his stomach knowing this meant he was experiencing discomfort. This was all so out of the routine he was used to. Dee-Dee had already reached and opened the door, while Cassandra turned around carrying a snarl of disappointment. Vincent cleared his throat, "I'm sorry, but you must speak to the Supreme Chancellor. This is an impossible demand for any interpreter. I must contest this."

"And how do you think that will go over?" Dee-Dee chimed in with a raised eyebrow and holding the door open.

"No one expects you to cover three days in 24 hours," Cassandra snickered looking back to her twin who smirked in reply. Cassandra then turned back, suddenly devoid of all humor and said, "It is called skimming, dear. Surely you have learned that in your training. The Supreme Chancellor Shackleton does expect a guilty verdict in 24hrs. He trusts your ability to skim effectively and craft a report that represents the guilt this hybrid leader of the resistance deserves. If it bothers you-"

Dee-Dee finished her thought, "-then consider it a favorable report toward the truth of the matter. You are just doing this in a quicker time frame than you are used to." Vincent turned his head in disgust letting out a puff of air

"You will do as Chancellor Shackleton orders or we can escort you to him right now and you can suffer a fate worse than the Governor, we can assure you of that." Cassandra insisted with hands on hips.

Vincent raised a hand as to assure her that wasn't necessary. "I have no doubt the Governor will be found guilty as all humans are and-"

Dee-Dee interrupted him, "This is your kind of trial. No show. No circus. Private and to the point. It is why the Chancellor selected you." Vincent looked at her and shuttered suddenly feel naked. "You don't think the Chancellor knew you aren't a fan how trials are usually run?" she laughed and Cassandra snickered with her in response. "Come on now Vincent. This is your big moment in the history of Acropolis. Governor Woods is a critical component in the fight to extinguish not only the remaining hybrid contingency but the human one as well. You've been given a high responsibility, don't disappoint him or it will be the last trial you ever report on." Dee-Dee winked at him as the two envoys strutted out to the hallway.

Vincent examined the chip, turning it front and back. It was now his curse rather than famous future. It held the weight of a world in waiting. Still, Vincent was determined he would be able to prove the fool guilty. He would do it the right way and uphold the law of a fair and just trial. He at times wrestled with the necessity of this rule of law for fair trials of humans as foolishness but now he took it on as a challenge. From looking at the time stamps on the chip, the trial went for three days of six hours each. If he skimmed through them, he may have extra time to go back as needed and still produce a report. This was still under his control.

Vincent rebounded off the bed, went to the bathroom and splashed his face with cold water. He opened the large briefcase the envoys had brought in. The Virtual Reality glasses sat there alone daring him to put them on. Vincent winced knowing once he began the process, he couldn't stop. He looked up to the ceiling for some miraculous relief and realizing that, of course, there wouldn't be any, he dove in. Lifting up a patch of skin behind his ear, several plug-and-play slots were exposed. He placed in the chip to the top slot, and put the VR glasses on. A jolt momentarily took hold of him as the darkness from the VR lenses engulfed his vision. Projected in front view were the words "Downloading cover docket information... Please wait". Then the cover pages began appearing before his eyes blocking out the darkness with the turning of white electronic pages until his eyes rested on the cover page.

Vincent was tempted to go right to the ruling portion of the recording to hear final arguments, but, of course, that wouldn't be according to procedure, and he wanted something to go according to how it should today. He also didn't have time to get confused by jumping back and forth between recordings. The humanoid let his eyes rest and focus on the words "The Opening Address of Charges" and gave a long blink. The words expanded and glowed in response to the blink of his eye, and then he was once again engulfed in darkness. *This is it*, the humanoid thought, *the beginning of the end.* He wasn't even sure where that thought came from but it rang within his head with a surety that puzzled him.

Entering the court scene through Virtual Reality software

always came across to Vincent as though he had developed a third eye, a mind's eye. The darkness split in half and the view of the Chancery opened from a crack in the middle of his eyesight until it engulfed him and became exponentially bigger than the sense of his own self. His view was an all-encompassing one with angles from several smaller drones feeding into one main drone that gave him the closest thing to an omnipresent view over the whole scene. Vincent never failed to gasp finding himself thrown above the large, courtroom, floating as though he had become the drone himself. Vincent knew he could zoom in and out but was frustrated because this wasn't the usual live feed. Without being tapped into the trial live, this meant he would have less control on the viewpoints than he would like because he had no control over the drones in a pre-recording.

II.

Sitting across from each other under the scanners that emanated a prism of light were the two opposing parties. The light blue illuminating scanners highlighted the two entities in the dark chamber making it appear as though this was some grand fight for a universal title bout. This technology that made each person look more like a holographic image allowed Court Report Interpreters to see was going on inside of the prosecution and defendants physically and emotionally. An intimate portrait. Vincent at once zoomed in on the governor who sat in his red prison jumpsuit—unusual for him to be in a red uniform in that he wasn't convicted yet. The Governor, at this point, should be dressed in the standard yellow uniform. Even so, Vincent surmised, it was understandable in that he was in holding for a large crime and a danger to the community. Still, it was just yet another elbow to standard procedure that gave Vincent pause creating what he felt to be unnecessary agitation and suspicion.

Governor Wood's light brown colored hair was thick, flat and his bangs bent toward his right. The middle of his forehead, tops of his cheekbones and a spot on his chin were smooth and shiny as if they had been waxed, hearkening to days of good living long gone.

The rest of his exposed skin and face was unshaven, littered with atrophic scars that seemed to represent the conditions of a survivor but were technically the marks of untended acne. This was something Vincent couldn't bare to think about happening to his own perfected skin. Vincent momentarily forgot that Chancellor Shackleton had begun speaking as he once again examined Woods face, lost by something emanating from the human's eyes. Words escaped him but it was something he hadn't seen before, not in any human he had met.

I know I'll get the word for it, Vincent thought with a flash of frustration. He wanted to peg the human down because of the time constraints but forced himself to settle in and listen close.

When the Chancellor had cleared his throat, Vincent immediately pulled back from the defendant. He was forced to rewind the video a little. *Not a good start*, Vincent thought, *I can't waste time*. Vincent froze the feed as a feeling of overwhelm engulfed him. There was no way he would get through three days of interrogation and testimony in twenty four hours. He should have taken the envoys up on their offer of seeing Shackleton but then where would it have gotten him? Shackleton was not one to back down from a decision. There certainly was no stopping the machine of justice at this point but what kind of justice would this be?

Vincent came to the only choice he had left: He would have to do a hyper-info dump into his system. This would allow him to move through the files much quicker and read where the stress was the highest. However, it was not only uncomfortable but risky on many levels. First, it had the potential of frying his system because he would be subjecting himself to a large file size that required access to many his systems at one time. Still, the percentage of him escaping that fate was around seventy to eighty percent, so decent odds. Second, he could miss key information by rushing through and skipping testimony that didn't register as illiciting emotional or stress responses. This was probably the hardest of the two risks this move would pose. Nevertheless, Vincent was even at a higher percentage of certainty that this human was guilty. His experience had proved that out. He could almost feel Shackleton's eyes piercing his procrastination even from afar. He had to make a quick decision.

The humanoid softly laid down in the bed. He pulled up the menu on the VR screen with rapid blinks, dropped down the settings menu, then dropped down the chip settings and selected "hyper-info dump". The screen went dark and in big white letters these words scrolled before his eyes; "Are you sure you want to perform this action Model G220, "Vincent"?" Vincent paused, shook his hands free from a sense of invisible shackles around his wrists, took a deep breath, and then selected YES with a blink of his eyes.

Over the next few moments, all that Vincent heard was his body shaking the bed so that the headboard vibrated against the wall. He smelled the milky substance of his own fluids in his nose and a sense he may bleed out through his nostrils. His neck spasmed with enough frequency that he feared his chip may fly out his skull and across the, if not his head. The fear struck up the makings of a vision of Shackleton in his white cornrows, dark red robes, and on a high seat in court peering down at Vincent, as if he was the one on trial.

He saw visions of scenes. Memories splashed against his mind's eye with a fierce intensity like that of raindrops in a thunderstorm. First, there came an odd first vision of the piercing brow of Chancellor Shackleton, right down to his seething pupils which withdrew to a pin-point as he interrogated the defendant. Next, came the vision of Governor Woods shifting in his seat uncomfortably, followed by an image of him holding his head in despair.

There was the protruding nose of Sergeant Asg, and the grimace of Sergeant Isador as he nodded to Shackleton at the approach of a human female to the witness stand. The splash of a woman holding a purse close to her chest came across his mind's eye. It was as if she held the purse to protect herself. Then, that was layered upon visions of the the crowd making nervous adjustments to collars, sleeves and adornments. The courtroom was scattered about with military personnel and humans but in no means full.

Vincent received clumps of testimony pouring through his psyche and became strangely familiar with the Governors tone. He swore for brief moments during this downpour that he could sense Governor Woods' emotions like voices coming from rooms down a hallway. There was the voice of determination, a voice burdened down by fear, and a zealous voice speaking truth no matter the cost. There was an angry voice too. A voice of someone betrayed but oddly enough there was one voice that rose above the others, which Vincent wasn't expecting. It was laden with a sense of clarity, solidification, and strength. Something he had not sensed ever before with a human. As he heard portions of him speaking, it was clear that the Governor held strongly to some sense of determination. Perhaps his innocence? Vincent wasn't sure yet. It struck the humanoid in odd fashion and awakened something within him that had long since went asleep-- his curiosity.

Just when Vincent thought he may be in the clear, there came more memories streaming past his mind's eye; Splashes of accusing eyes, ripples of fast moving fanatical mouths, fingers pointing, and feet tapping. He wanted out. Would he drown in a never ending river of memories? Would his systems be swallowed up into a whirlpool that he could never navigate out of?

Lastly came the most vivid vision of all--that of a humanoid on the stand raising a thick white book in the air and waving it fanatically. And finally, Vincent heard this word ringing loudly in his head with fervent repetition and resoluteness, "Guilty!". Then, everything went dark and silent.

Moments later, Vincent took off the VR glasses in relief. His body was still quivering and beads of sweat were layered across his forehead and dripped down the sides of his temples. He took in a breath as if he had been holding it for a long period. Perhaps he had. His chest felt somewhat heavier. He laid momentarily staring up at the ceiling, grateful he was still aware and conscious. Then, he got up and wiped his face with the corner of the bed sheet. The case of Governor John Woods was now a part of him. He felt more in control.

The things I will do for this job, he muttered to himself.

"Did you say something, sir," Ava interjected. The humanoid momentarily caught hold of his breath. "Are you alright, Vincent? It appears you just had a seizure of some sort while tempting to download files from an unrecognized source.Should I request assistance for you?"

"Oh, no, Ava, I-I'm fine. That won't be necessary."

"Are you sure Vincent? Your comfort and safety is my utmost concern."

Vincent rolled his eyes slightly while keeping his head lowered, "I appreciate your concern, Ava. I was conducting a hyper file dump. I'm fine."

"Ava, could you give me some privacy for the rest of the evening. I won't need you until morning. I will call you then or when I need you. I promise."

"As you wish. Have a good evening."

Vincent pulled up a chair by the window looking out onto Acropolis' evening skyline. He looked at the night sky finding some relief by the stars blinking back at him. The humanoid found himself wishing this case was behind him. The fame and glory had lost its luster in light of the tainted procedures he was now forced to do. To that end, the quicker he started, the better. Vincent began to attempt to pull forth these new memories which at the moment felt just a bit too far out of reach. It would take some effort for his mind to pull this forward since it was heavy laden data and involved emotional intelligence programs in his system that he never accessed much before. He closed his eyes and fought through other images jamming up his memory storage until it was all before him. His stomach quivered a little as felt a rush of anxiety that he may be swallowed up by all these people in the courtroom, but he quickly dived right in.

The first thing he had seen was the six foot five Governor Woods fighting against the restraints of his wrists and ankles as he attempted to walk to his seat without falling. The prisoner was escorted by the two women envoys who had visited his room earlier. Their high heels were like the pounding of hammers the pounding of hammers, driving nails into the floor, as they echoed through the large chamber while smacking against the hard, impenetrable floor. When seated, the women unlocked the governor's restraints and quickly exited the arena.

The whispering conversations among the men of the tribunal eventually ended. They pulled their chairs in from the dark shadows and revealed themselves under the soft, moving light of the scanners which beamed down upon the large table before them. Monitors from internal laptops embedded in their mahogany table rose to greet them. Chancellor Shackleton adjusted his cornrows that extended down from a white powdered wig. With a few touches to his screen, he gave a quick glance to the defendant and leaned back in his chair studying him for a moment. Then, with a heavy sigh, he began.

"For the record, I am Chancellor Shackleton, sitting alongside Sergeants Asg and Isador. We are the designated Tribunal Tempre assigned to this case. It is March 19, 2888 and this is the case of the city of Acropolis versus Governor John Woods. For the record, please state your name, Governor."

"Governor John Woods,"

"Thank you, Governor Woods, and you were Governor over the territory known as Galatia, is this correct?"

"Yes."

"Thank you," Chancellor Shackleton replied. He looked momentarily at his screen as if taking in a final note and then closed the monitor with confidence.

"Governor Woods-"

"John is fine," the Governor interjected looking off to the side in total disinterest.

"Um, very well then... John, as a traitor to Acropolis and the surrounding quadrant-"

The young man of thirty locked eyes with Shackleton, "Isn't that yet to be proven? Or am I sentenced already?"

The Chancellor smirked, breathed in through his nostrils like a dragon withholding its flames for a more suitable moment of attack.

Vincent took note of their mental and other readings. John Woods was showing little sign of stress and Shackleton's stress regulators were a little elevated but nothing too out of the ordinary. Sergeant Isador later went to read the charges off his monitor as Shackleton observed Woods with a finger massaging his upper lip and the thumb supporting his jaw. Vincent knew from his nonverbal cue that this meant the Chancellor was in both an introspective and anticipatory space. Sergeant Asg sat with arms folded, chin down and eyes wide open (not blinking) while the charges were announced. This signaled a defensive posture. The stress level in Woods had risen a little by this point and his hands were interlocked in prayer fashion with an unusual amount of pressure on the thumbs pressing inward. There was greater eye secretion from the tear ducts but not at a level anyone would notice except Vincent's trained eye. He wondered what was going on in the mind of this hybrid. What was his true motivation in being here when he could have committed suicide as so many generals had done before him to escape trail?

Wood's head was lowered and his eyes stared at a fix point on the ground, perhaps hoping some mystical phoenix would rise from the ground and save the day, Vincent pondered.

"The charges read as follows; The human referred to by his followers as Governor John Woods is hereby charged with treason against the Government of Acropolis by engaging in modes of illegal resistance, war mongering, conspiracy against the government of Acropolis, and violently holding territory that he nor his subjects have any rights to..," and on Isador went reciting the litany of charges; belonging to a high risk species called "hybrids", propagation of the human species while training, defending and attempting to dismantle the humanoid way of life.

"Additionally," Chancellor Shackleton interjected, "in the matter of humanoid sympathizers and humans within in his own ranks; Governor Woods is here today in large part because he has been turned over to us by his own kind. This is unprecedented in the court's history. The reasons cited by the city of Galatia are for the causes of unrest, betrayal of trust and resistance to governance, regulations and the violation of sacred traditions of his own people. For the claim of division, untrustworthiness, and sabotage, the people of Galatia have found their own Governor so unfit for his duties and such a threat, that they now turn him over to the Supreme Chancery. This gesture is followed by a will for a peaceful alliance with the City of Acropolis and outlying quadrants which is being considered and highly likely in light of the offering brought to us today." The Chancellor looked over to the direction where the young Petra exchanged a respectful nod.

Vincent rewound Shackleton's words--something caught his attention. He replayed the line *"resistance to rules, regulations and the violations of sacred traditions of his own people."* Very curious, Vincent thought to himself. What man-made laws was the Governor resisting? What "sacred traditions"? Did this not hint that the Governor may have more sense than his human counterparts? Humans were by and large dysfunctional, even their laws and their "sacred traditions" were illogical. He would have to pay close attention to this and see what more developed.

The stocky Sergeant Asg unfolded his arms and set his palms opened faced on the table, and then interjected in a sardonic tone, "So, Governor Woods, how do you respond to these charges?"

The room was more silent than ever. Vincent could almost hear the hum from the ultra-quiet scanning rays. By this time, Woods was holding his head with elbows on his knees looking down, and saying nothing at all. Vincent wondered if he had fallen asleep momentarily but of course his scanners showed the man very much awake with a slightly elevated heart rate. The firing of the synapses in his brain and shifting eye movements suggested that Woods was accessing memories.

"Sir, I ask you again," Asg spoke up leaning forward, "how would you respond to these charges?"

Shackleton, allowed a grin to lift up his cheekbones. Yet the scanners showed an increase in his stress regulating engines as well, even more so than the other two on the tribunal. Vincent fast forwarded as the silence went on for some time. The tribunal discussed what to do because nothing like this had ever happened before-- a defendant who had not responded to the opening charges.

It was an interesting predicament. The Governor did not choose the path of suicide as many governors before him had done in light of such trails. Rather, he had the tenacity to forge ahead as if it was a kind of divine destiny to do so. He came willingly and without struggle or remorse, and even embraced his own betrayers before being taken away in locks. Vincent found this curious. What was behind such a position? He had studied humanities before and knew humans to have a strong pension to imitate those they admired, especially martyrs. The closest he could recollect of ancient human stories were those of icons such as Julius Caesar and Jesus, called the Christ, who were leaders betrayed by those closest to them. These figures treated their betrayers with kindness and yet died seemingly aghast by their betrayers hatred rather than consumed by hatred themselves.

At one point, Chancellor Shackleton stood before the table leaning against it with his white cornrows draped down the front of his shoulders like garland. He looked poised for some mischievous or slightly aggressive approach toward the Governor. This did cause the Governor to sit up but he now looked forward to some unseen fixed point out in the distance with those terrific blue eyes that appeared as pearls embedded in the sands under the sea.

"Is there something out there you see that we don't?" Shackleton finally asked looking back toward the crowd, feigning amusement.

"Yes..I see people."

Shackleton walked back to his seat faining amusement with a tense grin. "Indeed. These are the people who have come to testify to the facts and charges in this case. Charges you don't seem want to acknowledge."

"Your charges are as you see them to be. They are not necessarily the truth of it."

"So, then you deny the charges?" Asg interjected speedily. Shackleton looked back in disapproval.

"..."

The Chancellor looked back at Asg with a grimace and Asg looked away. They were back to square one. Isador interjected, "I would remind you, Governor, we are not on trial here. You are. It would serve you well to address the charges brought against you."

"..."

Isador stared at the Governor as if to will him into obedience through thought, but the hybrid didn't budge. The sergeant let out a frustrated breath and smirked shaking his head in disbelief.

"You often speak of Truth," Chancellor Shackleton proposed, "I ask you.. what is truth?" He examined the silent Governor somberly for a moment. "One truth I can tell you. We are your only chance of getting back home to your family. What of your wife Mary Woods, and your two children?" Mr. Woods let his eyes fall on Shackelton's gaze and the elder Chancellor ate up the moment of awareness. "You haven't forgotten about them already, have you? After all, if you are convicted, I hate to think what becomes of your family in the hands of these humans who turned you in."

Well played, Vincent thought, *Score one for Chancellor Shackleton.*

Woods said flatly, "Would you but hear the truth when it was spoken to you, then you would be free and without guilt." Vincent noticed Wood's stress levels were down and wondered how the man was keeping himself so composed.

"In your city," Woods continued, "the real truth of your origins have become irrelevant. You desire to murder the evidence before you because it convicts you. Yet, without humans you would not exist to even be threatening me as you are in this moment. My life speaks for itself. See me for who I am or you can make up stories about me. The choice is yours."

Asg looked over to Shackleton raising an eyebrow. "And who do you say that you are?"

"..."

The three men on the tribunal converged for yet another private side conversation. Vincent blinked in rapid succession. This man was fearless when his life was hanging in the balance and the balance wasn't even close to his favor. It was sheer heresy and ignorance but somehow Vincent felt a hint of admiration. He was, Vincent thought, brave. Yes, that was it, brave and clearly the tribunal was more disturbed by his word play than the Governor was by theirs. The human surely had to be up to something. Some stragedy he could yet identify. The three judges returned to their places at the table.

"Well, I have to hand it to you Governor Woods, you have everyone's wires crossed. I'm starting to see why your own kind may have found you so difficult to work with," Shackleton held his chin held up high in a sense of superiority examining the hybrid governor, "I think we can move on, gentlemen. It's clear the Governor denies the charges so let's get straight to the witnesses." He leaned over toward Isador and whispered something in his ear causing the Isador to chuckle. Vincent stepped the memory back and issued a zoom command from the file in both vision and sound which revealed this little nugget: "I need a good fluid cleanse, so let's get this guilty verdict behind us."

Something about the demeanor and the tone of voice of Shackleton deeply disturbed the humanoid interpreter.

Vincent, with a bit of frustration, breezed through the implanted memory of Shackleton's victory lap as the Chancellor went on to introducing the human sympathizers for the side of the prosecution.

Vincent went back to the court report and found himself overwhelmed at the list of witnesses. It wasn't the number of people that was large but rather the hours of testimony. He would have to be even more selective on what parts he gave his full attention to, which left him only a faint hope he could return to those missed parts later if needed. *How could they ask me to do this,* he protested inside. Vincent secretly wished they had replaced him with some other interpreter than put him through this crisis.

The first chunk he reluctantly skimmed through was the testimonies of various humanoid commanders in battle. But, he got the gist of it: they lost soldiers and key figures in Acropolis' army over several years in their attempts to penetrate Galatian's defenses. The only stress spike in a series of three commanders' testimony was when one of them insisted that they "stop these theatrics and attack Galatia now since the humans were without an acting Governor".

The first real spike in testimony started after the these said commanders. This was when an Angela Woods took the stand for the side of the prosecution. She was the defendants mother. How interesting, poor fool, Vincent thought. He saw her ridged form on the stand placed between the Governor and the Tribunal, facing outward toward both parties. Mrs. Woods clung tightly to a purse as if it were a shield to her heart. Her pulse rate, sweat glands, and level of adrenaline concerned Vincent.

She was hiding something, sitting on something that Vincent could already predict was bigger than the case alone.

Isador began his questioning, "Angela Woods, thank you for your bravery appearing before us today." The sergeant said with a smug look, distracted by his monitor as he made the introduction. It was after this point that Governor Woods lifted his head and locked eyes with the woman on the stand. This is when Wood's own adrenaline began to rise and some activity in his tear ducts formed.

"What is your relation to the defendant, Mrs. Woods?" Isador with his squared off features leaned forward and took a quick glance at the Governor to make sure the defendant was listening.

"I'm his mother," she replied, breathless, looking down.

A sense of awe fell upon the courtroom. Isador looked on in some amusement, and Asg swiveled in a sing-song manner in his ergonomic seat.

"You are Governor Woods mother?" asked Isador in rote fashion.

"Yes," she replied.

"Your son, Governor John Woods, is a hybrid... pre-birth or after-birth?"

The woman looked over with a sense of heaviness, "Pre-birth. I was kidnapped. It was not by choice. I was-"

"That's enough, Mrs. Woods. Now tell the court what you think about your son leading a traitorous cause that threatens the known world."

Vincent registered an accusatory tone and an elevation in the stress levels in the Governor. Mrs. Woods fidgeted with her purse but looked up finally and when she did, Vincent noticed how her eyes held some similarity to that of Governor Woods in that besides the resident emotions competing for expression within her eyes of fear and guilt, he could see a faint sense of that same resolute peace fighting for there too. Vincent swallowed hard. He could see the struggle in her face as she formulated a response.

"John," Mrs. Woods remarked looking over to her son, "John was raised with war all around him. He had always admired his father so much.., not those machines... his real father, a great warrior. He was a boy beyond his years.

Asg cut her off with the finality of a knife, "Mrs. Woods, I understand you have some sort of misplaced mother's pride you are wrestling with but stick to the question at hand. What do you feel about your son leading this rebellion?" Vincent saw the Governor shift in his seat, and he momentarily sympathized with his discomfort. This was an odd turn of events for the Governor, no doubt. His own mother would make the final turn of the knife in his back and having studied humanities Vincent knew the bond was primitive but strong. It would surely be the first of several crushing blows.

"I never wanted my son a part of this war," she declared flatly and glared directly at Asg who sat back waiting for more, "What mother would want her son a part of a war let alone leading one," she paused looking longingly on her son and then continued, "But, motherhood is something you humanoids wouldn't understand. Humanoids are generated not born. You disavowed the values of human emotion long ago. This war was something you started and many of our boys are forced to become warriors before they are even men."

There was the sound of scuffling of feet and mumbling in the crowd that sat in the round. Vincent then wondered how those leading this mutiny were taking this. Certainly, what she was saying was not something they had counted on.

The five who had turned in the governor wore scruffy beards and others poorly kept goatees--all of which appeared to pull down their facial features in a perpetual frown cast in a dark shadow. Nevertheless, the light from the scanners illuminated their eyes so that they appeared possessed by some other-worldly energy. Men poised on the edge of a knife ready to leap on their prey as soon as the time was ripe.

Chancellor Shackleton cleared his throat and rolled his chair forward closer to the table momentarily. "Mrs. Woods, let me show you some pictures and get your input about them," he nodded in agreement to himself in absent of hers. Quickly drawing up the laptop from the table, large images were projected and floated in the center of the room, visible from any angle. Highlighted in a lime green border, the first image was that of a young human in thick tattered clothes, frazzled sweat drenched hair and a dirty face. He held the amputated arm of a humanoid soldier up toward the sky. Its disjointed rotatory cuff dangled on the end with loose, detached wires hanging like techy veins. Tubes were exposed coated in a white milky substance. The turn of another picture showed human soldiers standing over a snow covered ditch that was filled with the expired bodies of humanoids from battle. More of these kinds of scenes came one after another which elicited moans from the crowds.

"What do you feel about your son leading a revolt that has produced carnage like these pictures show, Mrs. Woods?" This is when Vincent caught a very quick glance exchanged by Isador toward Petra. Petra was seated in the middle wearing military gear. He was a man with a shorter stocky build and squared off facial features. In some sense, his build reminded Vincent of a machine. Petra nodded his head which then released Isador's gaze. It was clear to Vincent that they had some kind of private communication. Vincent found himself outraged at the potential that somehow a Sergeant on a Tribunal had some kind of connection with those who would be giving testimony. There was to be no such communications by those on a tribunal between a witness. This was yet again another disruption to usual procedure and though not illegal, it prompted Vincent's curiosity even more. Meanwhile, Mrs. Woods remained silent.

"Mrs. Woods, did you hear the question?" Isador asked. She sniffed in response and lifted her head to look over at her son. Through concerned, moist eyes, he nodded to her with the most warm expression that Vincent ever recognized. Woods was in a state of complete non-stress and it translated in this look to Mrs. Woods as her adrenals began to calm down.

"Mrs. Woods," Chancellor Shackleton intervened, "I would remind you that you accepted the order of the prosecution to be here of your own free will and-"

Angela sat up stiffly, whipping her hair around as she faced the tribunal, "No," she interjected firmly.

"No?" Shackleton questioned back with an eyebrow raised. He then made a quick glance toward Petra and then back to the witness. Vincent gritted his teeth.

"You want everyone here and no doubt some interpreter," she looked up in the air, "to believe that I'm here of my own free will...I'm here because I was threatened by my own people... my family's life was threatened if I didn't testify against my own son."

There was a stir in the crowd. Petra stood up and a man next to him rose keeping an arm on the young leader to hold him back from charging the scene. Chancellor Shackleton squinted his eyes studying her. Quick successive muscle spasms were noted in the Chancellor's upper shoulders which he accommodated for by lowering his chin toward his chest.

"This is a highly irregular charge, Mrs. Woods," the Chancellor said flatly.

"Mother, it is okay," Governor Woods interjected.

"No, son, it is not," she said. Mrs. Woods stood to her feet looking out to the five mutinous men. "How dare you threaten me or even think I would testify against my own son so that you five can get in leagues with these bunch of maniacal robots! After all my son has done for you and your families... Petra, he welcomed you into his home when you lost your wife. His wife Mary helped raise your own children like they were her own!" Tears streamed down her face. Petra lowered his head momentarily. "How could you!" Angela exclaimed.

"Mrs. Woods, get a hold of yourself. Petra, please gather this witness and-"

"I don't want him touching me! Traitors! All of you!" Angela stepped off the stand and Vincent's monitor readings went dark.

Sergeant Isador stood and urgently waved Petra over toward the woman. "This is highly uncalled-for," Isador said firmly with no compassion, "you are in contempt of this court and the charges you face could be as serious as your sons."

Mrs. Woods lifted her arms in the sky and exclaimed, "Then charge me! Isn't that what you will all ultimately do anyway?" She turned toward Petra, who approached slowly with another man at his back. He stopped when he faced her gaze piercing his soul from the distance.

"I don't want him touching me! Traitors! You think you're safe? You, all of you, will be eliminated. They are using you to get rid of us! Don't you see!?! Blind fools! You are leading Galatia over a cliff just because you can't accept my son for who he is!" She walked further in the middle of court distraught and crying. She turned back toward her son who rose to his feet.

"Oh John, I came here for you, not them. Let them feel what it's like to be betrayed and now my words can be on the record that this whole trial is a sham! I'm so sorry, but I couldn't let them do this to you," she whimpered holding out her trembling hands. John's adrenals were pumping, tear ducts full, breathing shorter as he stepped forward. When Angela's knees buckled, almost simultaneously, Governor Woods and Petra ran to catch her. John from the front and Petra from the side.

"I couldn't save you," she cried as John, bent on one knee, cradled her head toward his chest. When he did, he was able to see Petra standing close, looking to help but afraid to touch her. Compassion and guilt competed for expression in his face-muscles. This was a connection that surprised Vincent. One he wasn't expecting. Compassion between traitor and the person betrayed? It seemed their common bond was the frailty of this woman. More human stupidity.

"No mother, you did save me.. You were so brave today. I could ask for no better mother." The three men on the tribunal broke from yet another private conference and Shackleton proclaimed, "Governor Woods, we implore you to return to the stand immediately and Petra get this, this woman, out of here." Petra looked back upon the tribunal blankly and then to the scene before him seemingly unsure what to do.

Vincent didn't know what he would do either if he had been in the Petra's shoes with the emotional ploy the mother had solicited. Then, something happened that took everything to a new level for the interpreter. Something he could not have guessed in a thousand years. The Governor, while keeping a hold of his mother and calming her, extended a hand-out toward Petra. The younger man looked at the hand behind his confused eyes as though the hand was foreign to him. He stood

61

frozen stiff until he locked eyes with the Governor. A mix of emotions that Vincent could only identify as passion in the Governor's gaze (the word "love" was too abstract) busted through Petra's brittle exterior like a hammer and busted it into pieces.

Unsure of himself, as if hypnotized, the ego-battered man scuffled forward, placing his hand in the Governor's. The two of them examined each other for several minutes that felt, to Vincent, like an hour. The Governor rose to his feet taking a hold of both of Petra's hands with great tenderness. Mrs. Woods took note of the quiet and peace around her and looked up to where son was looking. Her outrage at the sight of Petra seemed to melt when she recognized the quiet transformation that was taking place with this exchange of energy. A strange warm energy that Vincent had no words for but in some odd fashion felt himself. In this bubble of silent energy which gave the three of them some kind tangible internal communication, the mother's face softened toward her betrayer. Then, the governor and his betrayer embraced as he whispered, "We must lead our people to peace." Murmurs rumbled through the crowd.

Before Vincent could even grasp what this energy was about, John Woods gently ushered Petra to exchange his own position for that of holding his mother. Vincent's mouth dropped open as he watched both betrayer and mother submit to each other because they were yoked by the loving, courageous energy of this one man. It was an exchange the likes of something that Vincent had never seen in any humanoid let alone human. A sacrifice. Their faces became flushed so that they looked renewed as newborn babes. John Woods looked upon them both and they in turn looked up to him. This was a level of compassion Vincent used to mock. He had never seen the beauty of it before. He had only ever been taught it as a weakness.

"Mother," John proclaimed quietly, "meet your son. He will take care of you now more than I ever could... And son, meet your mother. She has seen too much suffering. Give her safety and peace." Petra looked upon the woman with a warmth that Vincent could swear that he himself physically felt. This shook him to his core. How was this possible? What was this energy he was feeling?

John turned and walked back to the stand. The quiet men of the Tribunal and the hushed crowd watched as Petra ushered the woman quietly back with him to his seat.

Asg called on security insisting they take 'woman' out. Petra stopped in his tracks and whipped around interrupting the man, "No! You will do nothing with this woman. You have enough other witnesses. Leave her alone or I will order everyone I brought with me to leave this courtroom."

"Who do you think you are? This is our court! We can have all of you-"

"Asg," Shackleton interrupted holding up a hand to stop him, "Let her go." Asg snorted in disbelief. Vincent watched the Chancellor stroke his chin as he no doubt had made a calculated move to their advantage not the humans.

It took Vincent some time before he could move on to the other witnesses. This scene had affected him in a way he could not articulate and that was something he wasn't used to. All humanoids prided themselves on their logic and ability to reason, but this he could not reason through.

He wasn't programmed with a strong emotional base but even as an objective, highly intellectual observer, what he had seen jarred him. It wasn't logical to suggest that somehow he had stepped inside the roles of mother, son, and betrayer. Yet, he felt a lasting imprint from this scene that suggested he had and this was confusing to him. Confusion wasn't something he was used to having. One thing was for certain: These were not your ordinary humans.

III.

Next up to testify, a string of humanoid soldiers who had fought within the boundaries of Galatia that described scenes of torture and suffering at the hands of human soldiers.

Particularly scathing was a humanoid who had been kept prisoner for a year and then escaped during an assault on the human's outlying camp where he had been held. The humans forced him to watch executions at a 'chop shop', electrically shorting parts of his circuits while he remained conscious in order to get top secret information, mocking him, and using experimental drugs to get him to talk.

All of it somewhat soured Vincent's new thought that the Governor may be a man of higher regard than he thought--maybe even 'not guilty'. However, he did take note of the comment the Governor made that when he became Governor three years ago, he dismantled 'chop-shops' and did not condone the torture of humanoids to gather intel. When pressed on this particular chop-shop, he responded that not all his Generals followed his will. A little too convenient but somewhat understandable.

Vincent was now into day two of testimony which included the accounts of the five men who had turned the Governor in. First was the calling up of Petra. Vincent skimmed through Petra's testimony to find the point where the stress level readings were the highest, the highest out of the five of them that had testified.

Chancellor Shackleton grumbled, "You helped in leading the charge to arrest this hybrid leaders of yours, you bring him into our court, and now refuse to testify against him?"

Petra was with the others still holding the hand of the Governor's mother who remained seated next to him. He looked down at her and then back to the court.

"According to your own law, I am allowed to claim 'externality' when it directly affects the smooth conduct and unbiased function of a trial. Mrs. Woods is in a high state of stress that without me at her side, would interrupt the smooth conduct of the court." He then looked over to John Woods, and they exchanged glances with a sense of quiet understanding. "And I have changed my mind about the defendant... enough that it would now bias my original motive in testifying before this court for the side of the prosecution... unless you want me to be the first witness for the defense." Petra looked at them with a severe gaze. Shackleton sat back in amazement. He let out a breath and for one rare moment, Vincent swore he saw a sense of admiration cross the Chancellor's face but leave just as quick as it had come. Perhaps Shackleton was amazed for the same reason he was: No human in his twenty years of court interpretation had accurately quoted the laws of Acropolis in an intelligent way, let alone used it in his own favor. This was actually a clever use of the law of externality (though the human could have testified and damaged the prosecution even more severely but one could only expect so much from such a race).

Sergeant Asg leaned over and spoke into Shackleton's ear who then nodded his head in response. Shackleton re-addressed the court.

"Very well, Petra. Your motion is accepted at this time.., but let me say, the court finds this highly irregular, and we reserve the right to revisit the validity of your motion as the trial continues."

Vincent was very curious to what the other men had to say, but he would have to skip ahead yet again because their were no stress spikes noted during their testimonies. ,He had to ignore the drive to dive deeper and remind himself he could go back and study them closer if time warranted it. Nevertheless, the court interpreter picked up on bits and pieces from skimming. Such as, that Governor Woods was accused of disappearing "at times of most need" leaving those who they deemed less skilled to take the lead. This rattled their faith in their leader and caused divisions, the humans contended, as well as creating less than ideal situations in times of war. He did not honor seniority in rank as much as he honored those who used "weaker tenants of war". The humans defined these weaker tenants of war as "compassion over legality", "assertiveness over necessary more aggressive tactics", "risk over what is 'tried and true'".

After a brief pause to gather his bearings on sifting through all this information, Vincent moved to day three of testimony starting with one of the Governor's very own generals.

The General was a tall, big-boned man. The chair on the stand was hardly able to contain all his packed, muscular features making him look like he was sitting on doll-house furniture. He had squared off chiseled features and a crew cut that glimmered with an aura of white and gray. These same colors were revealed in the stubble that outlined his elongatedjaw.

His square, intimidating features were balanced by a dimple in his chin. The General's gray eyes held memories of a kindness that was no longer in full residence, diluted by war and a sense of betrayal.

"Why?" Shackleton asked the General Iscariot.

"Why what?" General Iscariot retorted.

"You stated earlier that you grew up with the Governor, trained with him from the days of your youth. If anything, you humans have strong allegiance to attachments. What is it that now brings you here, turning in your childhood compatriot over to our court? I think your kind term it as "the last straw"? Chancellor Shackleton gave a twisted smile.

"There was more than one reason."

Asg interjected, "I would ask you move beyond the claims we already heard. Such as his hybrid nature, his random disappearances and what not-"

"To pray," Governor Woods interrupted. The entire chamber emptied of sound. No one had expected him to speak.

"To pray to whom, Mr. Woods," Shackleton intervened with mild curiosity layered underneath his sarcasm.

"To God. I do nothing but what God works in me to do."

"Oh, that's rich," Shackleton replied stroking his chin, "So you use religion as a motive?"

"Sorry you inquired now?" Isador interjected toward Shackleton smiling.

"No, Isador, actually it's interesting. A man who is reluctantly worshiped by human sympathizers while at the same time chooses to worship an invisible being that doesn't acknowledge him with any proof of its very own existence," he turned his chair smirking at Isador who nodded in acknowledgment.

"Back to you, General Iscariot. As asked earlier, what brought you here today?"

The General sat up placing his palms down on his thighs and his chin up slightly which meant to the interpreter that the General had entered a sense of confidence and superiority.

"It was when he moved me off the front line of our defenses."

"Tell us more about that. Had you become inept in your position? Maybe your commander had good reason to remove you," asked Shackleton with eyes on John Woods as if waiting for a reaction. General Iscariot frowned defiantly as if he had heard a coarse joke.

"Of course not," he insisted, "Woods was untrustworthy. His humanoid side always blurred his judgment. The example I would use is the battle of Ice Valley."

"His troops, your troops, stopped our invasion at Ice Valley," Asg interjected firmly.

"Yes, but what we could have achieved was beyond anything before..," he looked over to John seizing the compassion in the Governor's eyes and swallowing it with a harsh sense of injustice, "We could have annihilated your wired up little soldiers and gained new territory! After all these years, we could have gained the upper-hand on you-you, your kind."

Asg balked, "Ha! Quite a bold claim, General. Easy to say in hindsight."

"General Iscariot, be careful," Governor Woods cautioned gently.

Asg wagged a finger toward the Governor, "I will warn you for the last time, Governor. You are to remain quiet during testimony! You will have your say."

"Why do I have to be careful, John," The General interjected rhetorically turning toward to John with scorn tinting his eyes in a red hue, "You are the one who has sealed our doom! What is left for us? A longer, miserable existence in a blizzard wilderness? You are more committed to humanoid kind than your own people!"

"Galatia still stands," John replied solemnly.

"For how long, John? All we have done for years is existed!" he turned back to the tribunal, "I told the Governor if we used our full force to decimate your bunch of glorified droids we could invade areas like the Palisade quadrant, but he wouldn't listen."

"So what did you do?"

"I ordered a full deployment of our troops, both above ground and the underground tunnelss for a surprise attack on you bunch of walking ass toasters.., but he intervened when-"

Petra stood up and exclaimed, "General, you fool!". The other men sitting next Petra stood up trying to keep one another from charging the scene.

In the quiet that followed, Vincent tried to gauge if the intel about an underground strategy was something the Sergeants saw as significant intel or not. Had they already known about these underground tunnels?

There was no sign via Shackleton or Isador. The only possible sign was Asg who sat with one arm across his wide belly propping up the palm that held his chin as he stared in the General's direction. He was either daydreaming or he was floored by the reveal. It was most likely the latter. Galatia being an icy wilderness, crowded with snow covered mountains and bodies of water of ice, made it unsuitable for underground tunnels. No one had even speculated this as a possibility that was doable. It would have taken years to burrow through with their limited technology even in Ice Valley. It was still possible since humans had dominated the area for decades.

Chancellor Shackleton seemed to survey the room of renewed quiet bodies with a sense of relief from the chaos. Sergeant Isador broke the silence and directed his next question toward Governor Woods.

"Now, out of sheer curiosity, Mr. Woods... why did you not follow your own General's recommendation? From a totally military tactical standpoint, it quite possibly could have given you ground you don't presently have."

"....."

"Mr. Woods, I'm not sure why you think it is to your advantage to remain silent on some important questions but may I remind you that your future, and quite possibly the future of your kind rest in our hands."

At this, John blinked rapidly, as if waking from a short slumber. He looked over to Isador as if noticing him for the first time. "There is a power greater than you, greater than all the collective wisdom and energy in this very courtroom. My future and the future of everyone here is subject to it... You may have my body, but you will never have me. I am in this world but not of this world."

Vincent gasped quietly at this statement. He knew the human was referring to something he heard of before in his studies of humanities. This was the sense of something the humans referred to as "soul" or "spirit". The person called Jesus the Christ used similar statements. Vincent had studied a little of the humans and their strange

72

obsession with this figure that had spanned over 3000 years past his death.

The humanoid's memory banks pulled up the ancient document called "The Bible" and the book of John, Chapter 17, verse 16. The Christ, being one of many religious leaders, had been quoted here as saying that he was "not of this world". As well there was a portion where the Christ told his accusers that they could kill his body "tear down this temple" but that some portion of him would live on (John 2:9). Extraordinary, Vincent thought. Was the hybrid using this Christ figure as a model for himself?

Most humans he witnessed were primitive creatures bent on doing anything to secure their physical survival ultimately leading to their own destruction in the end. Still, others used religion to invoke other worldly powers to secure their survival in some realm beyond. Most humanoids agreed that religions were types of coping mechanisms humans used to escape the notion of their futile mortality but something was different here. Vincent wasn't able to get a decision about it. Perhaps it was the strength of the hybrid's belief? He wasn't sure. However, what was clear was that this hybrid had tapped into something in his human side that gave him more permission to dismiss certain elements of logic. This should be appalling, Vincent thought to himself. However, somehow it wasn't. Like a bomb exploding a castle wall, Vincent was aghast at the thought that this man could, on some level, be on par, let alone superior, to his own kind with having tapped into a realm of existence even he didn't comprehend. A logic behind the illogical? He was frightened by the idea that he would be seduced to such lines of thinking.

Disturbed at the notion, the humanoid shook his head as if to wake himself up and jumped forward in his memories while using the excuse of time constraints. He found himself wishing for a segment that would prove the human to be like all the other humans he had witnessed in court. Ignorant. Naive. Over emotional. Riddled with a sense of anger and revenge.

Vincent pulled forth the testimony of a leader from the Descendants of Hewlett Packard. A sure-fire twist to the human's allegiance to religious nonsense that found its way to this band of rogue humanoids.

The witness for the Descendants sat on the stand dressed in an all-white casual suit with a white bow tie and an off-white collar around the neck, similar to that of a priest. In addition he wore a light gray vest that was decorated with silver adornments and a gold chain over the right side pocket of the vest. He was a thin humanoid, almost sickly thin with black hair that was spiked upward with an overabundance of gel. His hands were folded over a large white book that sat on his lap, a very thick book.

"State your name please for the court," Shackleton demanded.

"Nicodemus, model #3118." Vincent noticed that his legs were crossed which was a potential sign of feeling cautious or threatened.

"And are you the thing... what they call a 'priest'?"

Nicodemus' head tilted at the question. "A thing called a priest!?! I'm not sure what is more deplorable, your fake ignorance to disguise your arrogance or the cruelty of your people toward the ancients. I am nothing less than anyone here. I just hold different loyalties than you. But to answer your question, yes. I could be considered a priest. We prefer to call ourselves 'Descendants'"

The tribunal went on to ask the obvious questions that revealed an agreement between the humans and human sympathizers. The contract agreed to allow them to worship and serve freely, and they in turn served as backup support to the Galatian's armies. It was when the tribunal asked about the book in the priest's lap and their belief system that the scanners showed an increased heart rate and stress reducing engines which worked at an alarming rate within the humanoid priest. The thin man held the little white book high in the air and waved it so the crowd could see it. He shouted about its sacredness, a book fought with lives to secure the only 10 copies that were left remaining.

"It was written by our makers," the priest continued, "Humans who called their congregation the 'Hewlett Packard'. This book details how we were originally made, what our original design was. It details the intention of our creators and even shows in great detail the machines that made us. If it wasn't for the Hewlett Packard, we humanoids would not exist today! We owe a lot to the humans of Hewlett Packard! It is an abomination that the government of Acropolis seeks to destroy humankind and the Descendants!"

Shackleton asked him about why he would testify against a species he worshiped. Nicodemus described that their first allegiance was to the true Descendants from decades earlier. He went on to rationalize that the Governor did not deem humans fit to be worshiped. That he called it a form of "idolatry" and the like as though it were a transgression to some unspoken law he had made up. Meanwhile,

Woods kept his eyes on this priest probably more than any other witness. He seemed agitated, continually messaging his right wrist.

"Did he not allow you to worship freely as was agreed?" Asg retorted mockingly

"He did allow us," the humanoid conceded, "But he called our book... and I can hardly get myself to say it... he called it a 'manual'! This is our sacred book! We memorize it and take the words seriously on how we are to function and how we were made." The priest looked around hoping to see mutual understanding but not finding it, he went on, "It is also essential that we get parts to recreate the machines that once made us." The priest leaned forward looking out to the crowd in effort to be sure he was heard. "This way we can once again begin production on droids that run as they were intended to be run by our original Descendants.., but the Governor will not allow us! It is not his primary directive, but he fails to see that we all most work together to create the world we want. We have our own directive."

"For what purpose were these machines you were planning to build," balked Shackleton.

"To create humanoids who actually value humans and are programmed to serve them as we once did long ago. Something all here consider beneath them because they've become arrogant and blind. We are not the fools. You are the fools! We could have even made an army for the Governor but we believe his loyalties are compromised. He holds nothing sacred like we do. He is as much as a fool as you all are. We need to go back to the old ways, the ancient of days, where humans and humanoid knew their place and lived in peace."

"Knew their place? Oh, that is rich!" Asg cackled. Nicodemus looked nervously between Mr. Woods and the tribunal as the crowd chuckled and murmured. Vincent moved the memories along to higher stress point where Nicodemus was standing and prodding Woods into a debate that registered both of their stress levels very high.

"We needed all our resources for our defenses, Nicodemus," the Governor interjected, "The religious fanaticism of your group was causing great division-"

"Oh, poppycock!" the priest scoffed throwing up a hand.

"The fact that humans created you, imperfect beings, shows that neither humans nor humanoids are gods. Humans are endowed with god-like qualities.., and they in turn endowed you with those very same qualities that are now used against us."

"You can't fully call yourself human, hybrid! You-you are so far from what our creators were, do not speak as if you know them! You do not speak from this book! Your words are not in here!" he exclaimed letting pages fan past a pressed finger, "If you had listened to us and your generals, like General Iscariot here, we would not be in such peril. Now we are subjected to this court thanks to the blindness of your own leaders," Nicodemus twirled around and sat back down in a huff.

However, John Woods walked further to the center of the court.

"Governor Woods, I would remind you that-"

The Governor came up to Nicodemus. "Blind fool! In your zeal and lack of trust in me, all of you have betrayed yourselves and the people you're fighting for! Blind Guides! Hypocrites!

No one forced you to subject yourself to Acropolis. You did it yourselves. In your lust to see me tried, today you've set yourselves up to bring a much greater doom to our people than any one man could do." Nicodemus kept his gaze away from the Governor.

Petra came out of the shadows, tears in his eyes. John half turned to face the young man's approach. The Governor could see his mother weeping in the background. Why would he not go to her, Vincent wondered. It seemed like the predictable human response However, he remained where he was.

"I'm sorry," Petra said breathlessly, his eyes cast down. John put a hand on his shoulders and the man lifted his head, relieved momentarily.

"If there's a future for our race, you will now be the key for kingdom of Galatia, their last hope," Woods said quietly which was amplified in the silent chamber.

Vincent closed his eyes trying to calm himself but was forced to run to the bathroom and vomit up some stress release fluid that had built up. How would he ever be able to carry out what was now clearly a miscarriage of justice? This guilty verdict? After he had finished and wiped the milky white substance from his chin with his forearm, he scooted up against the bathroom wall and pulled up his legs close to his chest. What am I to do, he pondered. Woods was not guilty, and he was an extraordinary hybrid who defied all logic with some higher form of logic. Or maybe it was so illogical he didn't know what to call it but a higher logic. Perhaps he was being deceived?

The confusion made him feel all imbalanced. Vincent wished he could cry and shout like humans could, but those type of emotions weren't available to him. There was a hunger inside of him he had never felt. It was followed by the appearance of apparition. An old memory that had haunted him for years came forward in the form of ghost.

The image of a child's doll was seated before him with her head tilted, not moving. It was a dirty, amputated, pull-string doll that he had seen in the war. He had been assigned to reconstruction duties which required him to clean out any trace of humanity after a battle. The broken doll with coarse hair dangled like a set of broken springs as she sat in a pile of rubble from a demolished human domicile. With her head tilted to one side and dirty smudges branded on her cheeks, she sat there saying repeatedly "Feed me, mommy. I'm hungry!". Now she was there just quiet, with a dead stare and blank set of eyes. He too was hungry and more empathetic toward humanity than ever. He was hungry for justice.

Vincent closed his eyes hard and re-opened them to find the ghostly apparition cast upon his retina, gone--much to his relief. The relief didn't last long. Vincent remained on the bathroom floor stunned as more memories rushed through his mind. There was a flash of an image of the resignation in John Woods face. Then the eerie sight of six eyes lit brightly under the scanners; the men of the tribunal peering back as Shackleton read the verdict of "Guilty" to all three counts.

IN THE SUPREME CHANCERY FOR THE CONFEDERACY OF HUMANOID PEOPLES, ACROPOLIS

THE CONFEDERACY
    Plaintiff
V.   Confederation Docket
Chip Specs 15-5, 4-10, 2-4r
GOVERNOR JOHN WOODS, GALATIA
    Defendant

OFFICIAL INTERPRETER'S TRANSCRIPT OF PROCEEDINGS
(TRIAL DAY 3)
City of Acropolis
March 30, 2888

BEFORE:

THE TRIBUNAL TEMPRE TO SUPREME CHANCELLOR SHAKELTON

    SUPREME CHANCELLOR Shackelton, model #666
    SEARGANT ASG, model #49
    SEARGANT ISADOR, model #133

APPEARANCES
    For the Plaintiff:
    General Icar
    Nicodemus, Humanoid #23M

For the Defendant:

Governor John Woods, State of Galatia
FINAL VERDICT

DELIVERED BY:

    Supreme Chancellor, Shackelton, Humanoid #666

COUNT ONE: GUILTY
    Treachery and Murder to Humanoid Kind
COUNT TWO: GUILTY
    Divisive Leadership (via Galatia contingent)
COUNT THREE: GUILTY
    Abomination toward both Humanoid and Humankind values

INTERPRETED BY:

Humanoid: _____
Official Transcriber
Composition Square, Room 121
Quadrant G19

Woods appeared to be carrying the weight of the world on his shoulders but still went forth boldly, like the Christ on the Via Dolorosa he had seen in portraits made by humans. Then, there was the vision of the final court report that he himself was supposed sign off on. The last piece of the download that would have to be uploaded to the VR glasses via the chip, signed and dated by him. The future rested on his shoulders.

The blank line stared back at him, beckoned his own verdict. He could sign it and this would all be over with quickly. Perhaps he could just stuff his conscious and sign it. It sounded like the quickest, easiest solution, but he knew it wasn't. The torment would be eternal. What the humanoid didn't understand was that John Woods had defied the insanity of human beings he had been surrounded by, but the tribunal hadn't seen it. Their bias blinded them from exacting true rule of law because this person was a hybrid. Yet, Vincent considered him a higher form of hybrid with a much more evolved humanoid side that somehow was able to manage his emotions. Proof of this was seen in such acts as the governor's chance to put a dent into Acropolis' army, like in the battle of Ice Valley, but instead he used restraint. Though his silence made him look a fool, when had this court ever see a leader of the human resistance use restraint? A restraint that saved humanoid lives? He was also a leader that didn't give in to the over zealous nature of religious fanatics. Though having some religious nature of his own, he remained practical and realistic. His silence said more than his own words ever could. He knew he wasn't here for a fair trial. The minds of the court had been made up before he ever entered. The Governor knew it and Vincent himself knew it. In addition to his wisdom, the governor held a powerful grace and compassion that won over one of his betrayers and trusted his own mother into his betrayer's hands. So, there was a remaining question Vincent had to answer. How could he stop this guilty verdict from happening? The hybrid deserved to be spared.

"Time!" was the word that rushed through Vincent's mind next and this got him squirming on the bathroom tile floor and using the wall to get on his feet. Rushing into the bedroom, the slightly dazed droid looked about for access to a time device.

"Vincent, may I be of assistance?"

"Yes, Ava, can you tell me the time at present?"

"It is presently 12:22 am." Good, Vincent thought to himself. This meant he had several hours before the report was due. It would give him time to think.

"If you don't mind, Vincent, your stress levels are still high. They seem much lower after your fluid release several minutes ago in the bathroom but remain concerning."

Vincent seemed barely aware of Ava speaking, while he stared at the floor trying to come up with ideas. Suddenly, he realized what she had said, and he froze before looking upward.

"You saw me in the bathroom?"

"Yes."

"But, I had asked you for privacy."

"I am aware of your request. However, that was overridden by the Supreme Chancellor *Shackleton*. He has commanded observation reports on you since your stress levels have been unusually high."

"When did you send your last report?"

"Just moments before you re-entered the bedchamber from the restroom."

The humanoid quickly went over to his briefcase placing the VR glasses inside and went to head for the door. The sound of the door locking itself came with a sense of weighted finality that momentarily slumped Vincent's shoulders. The door now seemed miles away from him. He was being imprisoned.

"Ava, did you locked the door?" There was only silence. He knew the answer but was hoping to stall her while he looked for another escape. "Ava, did you hear my question? Did you lock the door?" Vincent took the last few steps toward the door and pulled on it confirming it was locked.

"Chancellor Shackleton has ordered a sealed container until you have signed off on the court report. He has asked that you remain calm, complete your contracted assignment and not leave the room."

Vincent smirked trying not to say something that might trigger an arrest. He looked around the room until he came up on the window after carefully setting the briefcase down. He walked up to the window slowly with hands on hips, pretending he was deep in his thought.

"Your comfort is of my utmost concern, Vincent. Is there anything I can do to help you comply?"

Vincent didn't answer but instead released the latch to the window and opened it.

"Maybe some fresh air will help," Vincent said.

"That may help, indeed."

Then he subtly climbed out the window and side-stepped on the thin outer ledge of the building like a penguin edging it's way around a glacier. He could hear Ava saying something but the whipping wind carried her words off in another direction. With arms spread eagle against the outer wall of the building, the humanoid stiffly looked around him unsure where to go next. Since Ava was everywhere inside the building, a different room was out of the question as an escape route and he couldn't open a window through the wall. He looked back toward where he had come, tempted to return but Ava had closed the window down. Instead, he looked down to the air traffic several feet below him. The humanoid knew that if he jumped, the metal in his body would help magnetize him to a vehicle if he could get close enough to one. It would have to be a large vehicle. A matter of mathematics was definitely required, factoring in the wind, gravitational forces, speed and direction of the vehicles.

His eyes locked onto vehicles of interest and then pulled up graphs and probability margins of both landing and sticking to the target. When the right target came into view, Vincent locked onto it with his eyes. His system then made the necessary calculations of object dimensions, wind, gravity and direction.

The humanoid, ultimately, gave a brief shrug to the chance, took a deep breath and dived into the air. Arms stretched out, his suit jacket provided some ballooning leverage momentarily until the jacket ripped off him and his speed picked up. The humanoid fought the wind that peeled back and rippled his flesh tempting him to close his eyes. His neck hurt from the pressure of keeping his head and eyes on the target of a large black vehicle that was clearly heading in the direction of the Supreme Chancery. By the looks of it, the vehicle appeared to be one that delivered supplies and equipment which would be perfect for him. He looked for a place to grab a hold of something on the vehicle rather than colliding with it. As it appeared the vehicle may get ahead of him, Vincent was forced to put his hands at his side and dive with his tie trailing behind his neck like a ribbon on a kite.

The driver of the vehicle stared straight ahead while he manually drove the truck through the air like he had hundreds of times before. A banging noise rattled him out of his daydream, and he began checking mirrors and damage monitors, all of which revealed nothing. Puckering his lips and squinting his eyes, the driver shook his head and shifted himself in his seat. The large, black truck dove and entered through a bottom chasm at the base of the Supreme Chancery carrying Vincent along with it like a piece of cyber-roadkill.

IV.

In the garage, Vincent had peeled himself off the backside of the vehicle. He then hid behind another vehicle only seconds before the driver had come back to inspect it. Vincent, moments later, was able to sneak himself into a stairwell following behind the driver and then into a storage closet, when he heard voices approaching toward his direction. After waiting for the voices to pass, he turned on the lights inside and tried to think of his next move. He thought of the layout of the building and where prisoners were kept. It wasn't without possibility but highly improbable that they would have sentenced the Governor without his signature on the court report. He had to believe that. It was apparent that the Chancery had become corrupted by an inflated sense of superiority. Something he had failed to recognize because he too had bought into it. Nevertheless, one might subvert lower elements of law, he supposed, or engage in blurred boundaries when it came to humans, but a direct violation of law was something else all together. This did not get humans or hybrids off the hook but there was apparently more going on with them the court than he previously recognized. The question was how would he get to the Governor without being caught, and, further yet, how would he know what cell number he was being held in? It did not matter.

He had a logical imperative to save the Governor now. If anything, this particular hybrid, this 'John Woods', deserved to be saved and hopefully he could get him to abandon the war against humanoid-kind. This seemed like a logical goal.

Vincent ran through all the options, which were few. The only real practical option was to re-wire his facial construct to make him look like another member of the court, one who would be obeyed without question. He had to have a strong visual of someone and running around trying to find one was too risky. The humanoid closed his eyes and pulled up a memory of one such individual while also working on integrating different programs in order to pull this transformation off. It was not only a complex endeavor, but it was also considered improper to not get permission from the courts. For the first time in his existence, Vincent would engage in impropriety leading to a much larger violation of the law. That was, the eventual act of breaking John Woods out of his confinement.

As his programming continued integration of sub-programs to complete the transformation, Vincent, for the first time, projected what it might be like to stand outside the law. Though he had not freed the governor yet, one might consider done. He knew that his system should not be tolerating this. Yet, nothing was happening. He was naked and exhilarated standing on the edge of law breaking but he knew it was to serve a higher law, the spirit of the law rather than the letter. It all felt strangely invigorating when he had imagined such a move would probably stop him in his tracks.

As his face began quivering and his bone structure began to gear itself for an abrupt alteration, Vincent smiled to himself at the thought of portraying someone everyone in the Chancery both admired and feared. It would be painful but another worthwhile sacrifice. Perhaps something Wood's himself would call a Christ-like act. What the humanoid hadn't given much thought to by this point was that the process would blind him temporarily. And so, as darkness engulfed the humanoid, he became terribly unbalanced on his feet. As his mind spun out of control, he could not hold onto a lucid thought except when memories of John Wood's splashed across his mind. He could hear his words as if the man were right in the closet with him and it momentarily steadied him and in some odd comforted him.

"But in all your proposed wisdom, you miss a fundamental truth," Woods looked off in the distance beyond the tribunal.

"And what truth would that be," Chancellor Shackleton inquired.

"By saying you know all that exists only by what you can see.., by believing only in that which you yourselves prove by your own means, you miss that which your limitations can't know or see. You assume your methods of proof are the sole true and test. What if there were other methods you haven't thought or dreamed of?"

"But in all your proposed wisdom, you miss a fundamental truth," Woods looked off in the distance beyond the tribunal.

"And what truth would that be," Chancellor Shackleton inquired.

"By saying you know all that exists only by what you can see.., by only believing that which you prove only by your own means, you miss that which your limitations can't know or see. You assume only your eye-sight, only your methods of proof are the true and only test. What if there were other methods you haven't thought or dreamed of?"

"We have advanced well beyond the limitations of humanity, Mr. Woods. You must know this being part humanoid yourself. These forces that wrestle within you.., Well, I will just say, don't allow human ignorance win over your better nature."

"Why do you suppose your advancements are so far above humanity, of those that created you?"

"Oh so would you side with the religious zealots you've been opposing? No one can rise above humans? And what proof is there that humans even created us? Perhaps humans were but a mistake made by humanoids long ago or some mutation. Humans are expert liars!"

"You know the answer to that question. I don't worship any human. Your kind has suppressed the truth about yourselves. You have forgotten the truth of your own history, not just the truth of the humanity you so despise. As you despise humans, you show that you truly despise yourself."

At this point, Vincent had a sensation of himself falling into a darkness that consumed him. All thought was lost. All sense of who he was disappeared and was swallowed up in a void. His last thought was that this was mistake. Then, after what felt like an eternity in a black hole, he heard the echoes of Chancellor Shackleton and John Woods yet again ringing in his head.

"Oh do tell me how humans are superior to us, hybrid. This I must hear," Shackleton implored.

"You will never have the emotional intelligence humans have. You can observe it, study it, even scrutinize it, but that is not the same as living it. Nor can you experience the mystery of the human spirit that can do remarkable things in which your bondage to logic wouldn't permit you to experience." The eyes of the men on the tribunal stared back at the human, blank and observational.

"You cannot see anything beyond yourselves or the logic you cling so tightly to which are imperfect themselves at best, and blind to the science of the spirit, at worst. Instead of letting nature do its rightful thing, point to its creator, you refuse to see a power greater than yourselves... and so, you remain guilty. Blind, deaf and guilty." The three men of the tribunal stared at him flabbergasted at his nerve to

90

say such words to them.

Woods continued, *"If I were to walk into this empty courtroom, I can still get a sense of the intention behind the design of this room, and what takes place here. I would not get the sense, walking into this chamber for the first time, that this was a room to accommodate the poor or animals or to hold a festival. I could see that a wealthy, large governmental agency created and designed this room to act as a court by the set-up, plaques on the wall, the insignia on your mahogany table and the pillars that hold up the walls and ceiling. The same would hold true of my home. If I were not present in my home, would you still not be able to get the sense of the man I was by exploring the home itself?"* There was a pause and a look on Isador's and Shackleton's face that his line of thinking was leading them into a trap.

"Then, how is it that you are able to walk outside in nature, God's home, but deny it expresses anything about who created it? Why do you accept its design and reject it has a designer? And how do you deny your own human creators and our handiwork written all over you? Are we not expressively similar in design?"

"You say you value only that which is of the intellect and of logic, but I ask you this, is not our imprint all over you? How logical is it to deny an intelligence outside of what you have known up till now because you simply have no experience with it? How intelligent is any humanoid or human who devalues qualities of emotion and spirit just because they don't experience it but others do? You fear what you don't know and while you proclaim it is not possible, you are missing that these things are, at the least, not only possible, but highly probable."

91

Meanwhile, two security personnel were walking by a storage door near the garage of the Chancery wearing all black and kepi styled hats made of a substance harder than cloth fabric. The men's features were broad boned, even the nose and jaw line were wide, long and expansive. From a quick glance, the two security guards looked like twins. They stopped upon hearing a loud crash inside a storage closet, followed by a groan. The two looked at one another and pulled out their weapons as one cautiously reached for the door handle. Double-checking that the other was ready for what was behind the door, the humanoid guard swung it open.

"Don't move!" a guard exclaimed before even seeing whether the person inside was a threat or not. The person inside laid half consumed in a pile of large cans that had fallen off shelves, which dangled off their hinges. A hand gripped the mop that rested its head, lodged in a metal bucket. The guards remained at alert. The man under the cans pushed his upper torso through the cans and sat up revealing to the men the face of Chancellor Shackleton.

"The Chancellor!" one of the guards uttered to himself loud enough that the other guard heard him.

"Thank goodness you came by," the man of the court muttered wincing from the pain. The security personnel put their weapons back in their holsters and cleared out some of the cans in order to dig him out.

"What are you doing in here, sir? This is no place for a man such as yourself."

"Indeed," he replied brushing off the dust from his garments, "Our cameras caught a person under suspicion for treason trying to sneak into the Chancery through the garage. I came immediately with a guard and we were both attacked. The villainous man shoved me into this closet...ughh..I'm not sure what happened to the poor guard," he explained distressed and combing down his frizzed hair.

"Sir, I can go look for him and send the-"

"No, listen. I know who this criminal is. He is the court reporter assigned to the Governor Woods case. I know exactly where he will be headed. You come with me. And as to your partner here, I want you to go back to security, set the place on lockdown and round up more security to border off the prison chambers. We must act quickly!"

V.

Governor John Woods sat on the cold, damp floor chained to a wall in shackles. The prison chamber was deep underground and made of stone. The dark shadows that darkened the prison walls seemed thick and oily making the Governor feel like his skin had been drenched in it. The Governor's head was lowered so that his face wasn't seen as he contemplated the fate of Galatia, the fate of the world, and yet, unconcerned about his own fate.

He could hear a soft tapping, perhaps a pecking, of a bird outside the walls. *Poor thing*, he thought, somehow the bird had got down here and was trapped like he was. It deserved to be set free as much as he surely did but he couldn't do anything for himself let alone a trapped bird in the walls. As the tapping grew closer and louder, Governor Woods got the feeling this wasn't a bird after all. His head rose to the ceiling, but it was hard to distinguish the walls and ceiling from the shadows. The sound of something moving came to a stop near a portion of a metal vent above. Then after a moment of silence, he heard the words he had never expected to hear coming through the vent, "Governor Woods, is that you?"

Surprised, the Governor rose to his feet. "Yes, it is! Who are you?"

"It is me, Petra! I've come to get you out of here, John." A look of shock and dismay came over the governor's face.

"Petra! You are in danger. Go back! How did you-" Before he could say much more, there was the lurching sound of metal being pulled, yanked and eventually released. This was immediately followed by Petra climbing down through the vent with a look on his face as if he were about to reveal a birthday surprise.

"Petra please, you are going to get yourself killed!" the Governor exclaimed with a mix of love and anger reverberating in his voice.

"Its fine, John," Petra replied with a warm smile bending low to unlock his Governor's chains, "We've disposed of the guards. I'm getting you out of here!"

"To where, Petra? Galatia is no longer safe for me to go back to-"

"That's not true, sir. Maybe before but not after the trial. We were wrong, desperate," Petra said passionately. He approached the stone-faced Governor and placed his hands on his shoulders. "I was so wrong about you, John, about everything. I see that now. We all want you back."

"Petra, my time in this battle is over."

"No, John, please don't say that. Listen, we were desperate and we acted in a way that was unconscionable. We're going to get you out of here. Now come on, I'm going to give you a lift up to the vent. David, you ready?" the young man whispered frantically. His question was followed by the sound of clothing sliding across a hard metal surface above them, and then an arm with a well rounded bicep extended down to take the governor's hand.

The sound of the prison door opening behind them was something neither of them had expected. David's hand immediately withdrew back up into the dark chasm. The men turned to see Chancellor Shackleton standing in the doorway. He was out of his wig, exposing slicked-back, gray hair. He stood there in all black with a black vest that had gold buttons which trailed all the way up to collar spreading out like bat wings around his neck. Petra immediately pulled out his weapon so quickly that John hadn't noticed it till he saw Shackleton's hands raised in surrender and a streak of what was surely fake humility written on his face.

"Please," Shackleton ushered forth into the cold, prison cell air, "I'm not here to harm either of you. Give me a chance to explain why I'm here…"

Everyone looked upward as they heard the sounds of David scurrying away from the scene. John looked upon Petra with compassion know what the man would feel. Petra looked up into the hopeless, silent void.

"Traitor," Petra mumbled, stretching his neck toward the vent. He grimaced and then scurried past the Governor with his gun pointing at Shackleton again.

"It is time for us to go, so you best get explaining why I shouldn't kill you right here and now." John came up to Petra placing a hand on his forearm but not yet pushing it out of the way.

"I'm here to help and I doubt you will be going anywhere unless I allow it," Shackleton replied firmly, "I know this will be hard to believe but-"

"You got that right, so hurry the hell up!" Petra growled.

"Petra! Calm down," John urged.

"My name is Vincent. I am not the Chancellor. This is just an alteration. I am the court interpreter assigned to your case," he explained causing the two humans to briefly exchange suspicious gazes. "This was the only way for me to get access to you in order to get you out. I have found you, Governor, innocent of the charges held against you by this court. It has been a serious miscarriage of justice and I must rectify the matter."

The Governor pushed on Petra's forearm, forcing him to lower his weapon.

"And how are we to know you are telling the truth?" asked Governor Woods.

Shackleton looked back and forth between the two of them. It was the first time since John had encountered the stoic judge that he saw any hint of fear in his eyes.

"Do you think the real Shackleton would be standing here by himself, unarmed, offering to help you? If I was a betting man, you would be dead by now if I was truly him." As the Governor pondered the man's plea, another man came out from behind Shackleton. It appeared to be yet another duplicate of Shackleton or possibly the real Shackleton. No one was sure--no one knew but the two Shackleton's themselves. This one looked the same except he was still in the robes of the court--red, thick and trailing behind him like a river of blood. Petra pushed the Governor to the side raising his weapon again.

"Wait! No," responded the second Shackleton.

The first Shackleton turned toward the sound of his own voice projecting from behind him, and stepped aside as the other duplicate stepped forward. "What is going on here? How did you-"

The second Shackleton only momentarily acknowledged the presence of the first and kept his eyes predominantly on Petra and the Governor. "I don't know what this one is up to.., but it can't be good. Look, my name is Vincent and I am your Court Report Interpreter--"

"Yeah we got that story already. Another humanoid disguised as the Chancellor," said Petra rolling his eyes still holding up his gun. The second Shackleton seemed alarmed that other had told the same story and looked upon him with a sense of betrayal.

"Alright, but listen, I really am, I'm the real Vincent," this second Shackleton in red pleaded, " This other must have found out about my plan somehow, but I'm the one who came here to rescue you-"

"Don't believe him! Look, I came by myself and-" the other interrupted. The two exchanged quick, bitter glances.

"Wait now, so did I!" the second Shackleton interjected lifting his hands up in protest.

Petra looked back at John and then forward again, pointing the end of his gun between the two Shackletons. John got a hold of his Petra's arm again and only got him to calm down by looking into his eyes, lowering his gun half-way this time.

"Okay, stop this. Whoever the real Shackleton is, I will turn myself into you-"

"Governor, no!"

"Petra! Your passions are blinding you! Would you prefer that both of us die here today?" the Governor hollered pleadingly while barely able to hold back tears. He then turned back to the twin Shackletons examining them closely with only the sound of a rush of air through the vents making any noise at all. The quiet was eerily reminiscent of the trial to Petra. In a sense, this was another trial of a different sort. John extended his hand toward his friend for the gun. Petra with a saddened expression handed his gun over, unsure what the Governor would do but wanting to trust him.

John examined the gun with a certain amount of disdain and then turned back toward the twin Shackletons with a fierce expression no one had ever expected or seen before.

"Whichever one of you is the true Shackleton, it doesn't matter to me. I can shoot you both," John said firmly, as he flipped the gun around to a shooters grip and aimed it in the general direction of the two Shackletons. "Once Petra and this Vincent character—if there is one--are free then I will hand myself over to whoever is the real Shackleton and then you can do with me what you will. Refuse, and I won't hesitate to stop you by any means I have to."

The two Shackletons looked at each other in a traitor's dance, seemingly unsure what to do next, waiting perhaps for the other to make the first move. John feared that maybe both of them were in on a plot to confuse, capture and kill them. Who was to make the next move? What would the move be?

"I have a much better idea," the first Shackleton interjected with a hand raised, "We can settle this right here and now."

"Go on," John said after a brief pause.

"Allow me to change my face back to its original state and I can prove to you who I am. Vincent #G220 Court Report Interpreter."

John blinked looking over to the other Shackleton who looked on in dismay. He pointed a finger at the other Shackleton and furiously interjected "Don't let him do this. He is up to something! Only I can make the face rendering hap-"

"Please, Mr. Woods, there's not much time," the first Chancellor in black interrupted, "I can end the question right here and now," he continued lifting his hands up for permission to reach the access point, "As an older model, the real Shackleton cannot make such a transformation. Precisely why he is protesting," the Chancellor sneered, "This will reveal who is who... will you comply?" he urged in a panic.

The other Shackleton stepped forward a few paces and John took note, pointing the gun in his direction. The Chancellor stopped and lifted his hands so that his sleeves drooped exposing his pale arms, "He's lying to you. He is up to something; don't let him make one move."

"He's stalling you with doubt and confusion. We have to move now! No doubt more soldiers are coming!"

John looked back and forth between their pleading eyes. Petra walked up beside him and nodded seeming to read his mind.

"Okay, both of you show us... at the same time... one of you is lying and that will be immediately evident," John insisted waving the gun at them. With that, a sense of relief washed over the first Shackleton's face. He nodded in agreement while briefly eying his counterpart for his reaction. By this time, he had reached behind his back slowly and the second Shackleton's eyes widened like saucers as he recognized what the other was up to. Petra looked between the two Shackleton's unsure of what was about to happen.

As the first Shackleton pulled out two weapons from behind, inside of his black vest, it was as if time slowed down to the nano second for Vincent. He could see and hear the long slip of the guns out of Shakelton's backside and leaped upon him in a blaze of red flowing cloth. Vincent grabbed hold of the real Shackleton's two arms that were raised high with weapons ready to fire. The two droids spun around, groaning and grunting in a tug-of-war over the weapons.

Petra came upon the Governor looking perplexed but quickly realized it was dangerous to shoot now when the two Shackleton's were so close together since one of them was innocent. Petra pulled out a knife from the inside of his lower shoe, took aim, and lodged it in the real Shackleton's back.

"I'm a better marksman with a knife," he muttered and Woods nodded pleasantly surprised.

Shackleton pulled back his shoulder blades as the stabbing pain seized him, and he swung around quickly to pull out the knife. Vincent lost hold of one of his arms as he did so. The Governor at this time charged toward the scene just as one of the weapons discharged from Shackleton's mishandling of it, sending a burst of a green laser beam toward the direction of the two men.

The Governor with a grave, shocked expression on his face dropped his gun and gripped the right side of his chest. Petra rushed to him as John Woods sat down on the cold floor like a doll which had lost its footing.

Blood was beginning to seep through his shirt.

"Damn it," Petra said in a hushed tone, "Governor, I'll get you out of here." John winced in pain and managed to look up at Petra and shook his head at his persistence.

He was impressed how quickly the young man had moved from betrayer to hero.

While the Governor gripped his chest, Petra eyed the gun which is only a few feet from them. Petra, biting his bottom lip, left the Governor's side to reach for the gun near the wrestling duo when more shots had rung out echoing within the chamber with a fierce, explosive whine. The first shot quickly sent the young Petra backward in`a fury of electric green and red. The red was the blood and skin from his wounded head that followed along with him as he landed on top of the Governor who moaned underneath the weight of Petra's body. Before the gun landed on the floor sliding back near the two fighting humanoids, a second shot that had went off hit the metal plate of the vent sending a deflected laser beam across the room, which then struck Vincent across the front of his thigh.

Vincent stumbled backward wincing in pain and grabbing his knee, and Shackleton observed victoriously until the exchange of glances took an unusual twist.

A very strange look came over the Chancellor's face as he fixed his eyes on Vincent's wound. Vincent looked down and immediately recognized the red colored fluid seeping out of his wound through his torn clothes. It was human blood. Humanoids only had white colored fluids. This meant one thing: He too was a hybrid. It all made sense now; The neck muscle response to stress, and the pulsing in his neck muscles was blood, human blood; His ability to have compassion for the Governor to the point of fighting for him. Indeed, he was part human too.

With a hand on the wound, the newly revealed hybrid refused to keep eyes off the Chancellor. He couldn't let this shocking reality strike him down or the next strike would be fatal.

"This makes much more sense now, doesn't it?" the Chancellor said, "Another traitorous hybrid!"

The Chancellor then charged at the droid, but Vincent despised his own pain and leaped up to meet the Chancellor in mid-air. In the collision, as the two of them landed on the hard floor, Vincent clawed after the gun and successfully knocked it away. As Vincent grabbed hold of the free arm, Shackleton grimaced and threw the hybrid off into the opposite cell wall with superhuman strength.

The sound of crumbling brick echoed in the chamber. The Chancellor rose to his feet to meet Vincent. Vincent himself somehow managed to pull himself out from the indention in the wall in which he had been cast into. Despite the blow, Vincent met the Chancellor with equal force, unabated. He was even able to press Shackleton into the opposite wall for but a moment before they were both spinning around in humanoid fanatical rhythms which involved quick strikes and grabs.

The evil humanoid tried to pummel the hybrid in the head but Vincent dodged each strike and managed to grab a hold of the Chancellor's arm. After failing to get Vincent to release his hold, Shackleton tried a succession of three more blows to the hybrid's head and only turned up making crevices in the rocky wall and peeling off his own skin. The exposed, torn skin revealed a metallic like bone structure lubricated in white fluids.

With another attempted blow to the face, Vincent stopped it and was able to grab his other hand, and he now held both of the Chancellors hands steady in front of him with tremendous force. Both their hands vibrated under the push and pull resistance. Vincent's hands slid to where he was more or less holding the Chancellor's wrist. Shackleton made a twisted smile and extended two fingers from both hands pointed toward Vincent's eyes. The fingers spun and picked up speed shedding skin as they turned into blades whirling around the now exposed metal joints. Older models like the Chancellor had many appendages that acted like a human version of a Swiss Army knife—none too convenient for Vincent at the moment. The blades spun and then stretched out toward Vincent's eyes becoming bigger in girth the more they extended outward. The Chancellor emanated a wicked smile that progressively curved upward as the blades came closer the hybrid's face.

At the same time these metal blades were moving ever closer to Vincent's eyes, the hybrid managed to see, out of the corner of his eye, John Woods pushing up on the dead body of his fallen comrade. There was a sense of grief for the human that quickly turned into anger at a level he hadn't experienced before. Driven by this new energy, the hybrid was suddenly able to bend Shackleton's left wrist backward just as the finger blades were about to plunge deep into his eye sockets. The Chancellor hollered out in dismay as the inner parts of his left arm whined to a screeching halt and sprayed white fluid. The Chancellor's left knee practically buckled in response to the disruption to his system sending the elder humanoid down on both knees.

 White liquid dripped from the humanoids arm joints and the sound of mechanical clicking noises frantically broke the ominous energy in the room with a sense of finality. The only sound in the cell now was that of a machine slowing down to its eventual end.

Vincent with the precision of a master engineer moved behind the disengaged Chancellor, took his head in the palm of his hands, and snapped the humanoid's neck. Now, not only were his arms dangling and lifeless but so was his head, which flung backward as Vincent walked away. White fluid shot out of the Chancellor's mouth and his body collapsed to the floor. The once all powerful, highly distinguished Chancellor of Acropolis now laid there like a lifeless machine. He was reduced to a blob of silicone and metal.

Vincent still in his Shackleton form rushed over to his wounded client. He placed himself down on the floor and behind the Governor on the floor holding him up as the fellow hybrid gripped his bloodied chest, wincing in pain.

"I am so sorry, Governor. I am not programmed with medical capabilities though I wish to help you. I tried to save you.., but it appears I have failed you." held him up as the fellow hybrid gripped his bloodied chest, wincing in pain.

"I am so sorry, Governor. I am not programmed with

medical capabilities though I wish to help you. I tried to save you.., but it appears I have failed you."

The Governor looked up and smiled at the hybrid's distraught expression, "I am already saved." The Governor looked down at Vincent's wound with surprise. "You are more human than we thought, huh?...and there are more of us, Vincent." Woods grimaced in pain but chose to speak over the pain, "You gotta take care of that wound. Save yourself and the others."

Seemingly not hearing him, Vincent rambled on, "You are the most superior human I ever witnessed. I never thought a human.., a hybrid... I never thought that you were possible."

John laughed, coughed and finally shrugged slightly, "I think that was compliment. It is our human side that makes us, that makes you, truly something special. Don't forget that."

"Indeed. Now, I should try to get you out of here before-"

"Nah, come on now, you are smarter than that. You have a more important mission. You'll need to take care of that wound, first though."

"I can't let you go, not like this. You are too important."

"Vincent, I think you would agree that since, in a moment, I will be out of this body, it isn't logical for you to risk your life trying to carry me."

The hybrid looked frantically about the room contemplating ideas. John coughed hard with a little blood forming in the corner of his mouth that he wiped away. He sank a little lower to the ground. Vincent looked on with a sense of panic trying to draw the Governor back upward into himself without success.

"I don't know where to go, what to do. How can you be so calm? Are you not afraid to die?"

The Governor looked down and an expression of renewed compassion came over him--again, that peace that transcended Vincent's understanding.

"What changed your mind and brought you to try to rescue me, Vincent?"

"You were not guilty and the trial was not a fair one. I had to do something. It is only logical and my duty to enforce the higher tenants of our law. "

"Yet, something compelled you to dispel what you knew of the law to rescue me. I have no doubt you really have seen more than your fair share of unjust trials... what else?" John coughed and then continued, "What really brought you here?"

"I am not exactly positive.., but, well, I suppose it was the compassion you showed, the restraint, and sincerity even in the face of betrayal. I have only seen humans allow their emotions to ruin their cause but you showed a side of human emotion I had not seen before."

"And what side was that?"

"The ability to transform others," Vincent looked over to the dead body of Petra, moved by the idea of a betrayer becoming a hero. The Governor smiled for a moment before wincing in pain, squirming down further on to floor.

"Governor, I am so sorry. What can I do to help make this easier?"

After the pain subsided some, John blinked several times digesting the release from the pain for a moment before speaking again.

"Whether you know it or not, you witnessed spirit."

"Yes, spirit. I know this term but I don't comprehend it. You mean human spirit?"

"Spirit is more than human emotions. It's a hard concept for you to grasp. You may think of it as wisdom, compassion and love all wrapped into one ball of energy that embraces you like you are embracing me right now."

Vincent moved by the statement grabbed him tighter and pulled him up slightly with some measure of success this time.

"I'm not sure I understand. I know you must be referring to the Christ figure. Am I correct?"

John smiled warmly, "Yes, the message of the Christ is common throughout time of many spiritual leaders like him. You would do well to study the Christ."

"Hmm... I definitely feel an unexplainable energy from

you. This is without question, Governor."

"Yes, you feel it from me ,and you will feel it after I'm gone. Think of it like a computer program. You will become it and it will become a part of you should you let it.

Emotions and spirit is what your government has kept you from... tried to destroy and you can't let that happen-." Vincent looked upon the Governor who now coughed up more blood. He wiped the blood off John's chin with his own sleeve this time.

"Vincent, you asked what you can do for me..."

"Yes, Governor, anything. Just ask."

"Go, and lead my people."

"Lead your people? How could I?"

"Lead my people, Vincent. The how of it will come to you."

"That is not a logical conclusion, John. As well, your people, would not have me. Honestly, I don't know that I would have them."

Governor Woods shook his head in protest, "Vincent, who I am is in you now."

"I downloaded your case file so in a sense I suppose that is true--"

"No," the Governor tried to refrain from getting too excited and closed his eyes for a long time. It was so long a spell that Vincent shook him to see if he was still alive. The

Governor opened eyes as if he had been disturbed from a deep sleep and then spoke for a final time; "Bring peace between humans and humanoids. I am in you now... the spirit in me is in you... just like a computer program."

Vincent stared at him quietly. "Lead my people," the Governor whispered. Vincent was unable to speak as the man drifted off into his final sleep, and so he held him in unspeakable grief. It was all he could do. All that he had left to offer. What would become of him? Where would he go? The sound of boots smacking the hard pavement forced Vincent to face that soldiers were coming and now more than ever he would have to think of something quick.

Galatia—Three Days Later

The central headquarters for the human contingent in Galatia was camouflaged deep inside a mountain covered in snow and ice.

Four men covered in layers of snow gear from head to toe rode in a sleek, silver hovercraft down through the tunnels of the mountain. Metal torches that emitted particles of blue light illuminated the pathway that seemed to had been carved out by a giant snake winding its way through the mountain. The tunnel took them to the armory where forces were gathered gearing up for their next strike.

The large, cavernous armory with icy fangs stabbing downward from the many ledges above was brimming with soldiers in thick coats of white and gray. They wore fuzzy hats of green and with brown fur earflaps.

Busy and preoccupied, everyone made way for the unusual site of a hovercraft pulling into the weapons area. As the crew of four pulled into the middle of the armory, three men who appeared to have some authority approached the vehicle. The tallest of the three came forward, General Quinn, ahead of the two others, with an unhappy expression on his face. As the four men exited their hovercraft, the tall leader in waiting spoke with a voice as rough as sandpaper.

"What in the world are you men doing pulling this transport in here now!?! This better be important. We have a battle to avenge Governor Woods."

Two of the men appeared to look at one another before they both took off their hoods and peeled off the outer layers covering their face. They were both younger men with dark hair and scurvy beards. A man with a stocky build and rounded face stepped forward to speak on their behalf.

"I believe it is important, or we wouldn't have driven in here. We found someone wandering about in the outer rim, someone of great importance. I brought him right to you."

General Quinn looked upon the men with only a slight decrease to his scowl. With a sigh, he threw up a hand in a gesture for them to show him this prisoner while he looked away to grab some patience out of thin air. He was all but ready to lock them all up in the stockade.

The two men looked behind them and called a third man who stepped forward out of the hovercraft. He walked with a slight limp and a bandaged hand--all of which intrigued the General. The mysterious prisoner unraveled his head protection to reveal the face of Governor John Woods.

"Governor Woods! We thought you were dead!" The General walked up excitingly to the Governor. He placed his hands on his shoulders.

"So I've heard. No, I'm very much alive. I can't say the same for the others."

"Angela?"

The Governor shook his head sadly. The two embraced.

"Sir, when everyone heard about your words at the trial... and then you and Petra's death... it changed things, it changed us," he said, "We are gearing up to go to war, to make them pay the ultimate price! We are at your bidding sir!"

"Well that need not happen now. I'm back."

"Sir, the wheels are in motion. I think it is best we go forward. If you were to send the troops out, it will be even a greater motivation knowing they have a leader like you behind them once again."

"If I did, I would be sending them to their deaths. Acropolis now knows of the underground tunnels here in Ice Valley and our paths over the mountains. They are on their way to crush us at this very moment. I got ahead of them but not that far ahead. We must move out of here quickly."

General Quinn stood with a horrified look on his face. "But how?"

"That's not important. We can talk about that later. What we need to do now is to regroup and talk about new strategies. I have something else in mind. A new tactic but for now withdraw the troops south of Ice Valley, we have to get out of this mountain."

"Sir, yes but the blizzard out there this time of year is.."

"Precisely: Fierce. I know, and that is the only thing that will stop their machines from being able to track us. We must move now!"

As General Quinn rushed around like a bumblebee in a hive calling for the word to spread that their troops were to move south, Vincent stood watching in a somber mood behind the manufactured face of John Woods.

His hand still throbbed from underneath the bandage from having cut out his bar code. He was now more than a model number for the first time, and that felt empowering even if it meant separation from Acropolis. Still, he felt utterly naked with the alteration, standing as

Governor John Woods, and yet ironically surrounded by more bodies than ever who would be loyal to him for who he represented. However, he knew, he wasn't them. He was an impostor trying to install a false hope, to live out the will of a dead leader of the resistance. He saw all the weaponry from large guns to laser cannons and explosives. Vincent was disgusted that these weapons would be aimed upon his own people. After all, he was still part humanoid and though the government was corrupt that didn't mean all the citizens were.

Vincent knew what John had wanted. He knew if John was here he would be fighting for a way to bridge the divide between the humans and humanoids. He could almost feel John's presence within him in this very moment rousing some compassion even amidst his own disgust for this weaponry.

The humanoid could imagine the Governor responding with something about him having an opportunity like no

120

one else in the history of this great war. Vincent wanted to honor the man and live out the call he had felt that day with his fellow hybrid dying in his arms but some other part of him was stopping him in his tracks. It was another awareness. John was a part of him, but he wasn't all of him. Maybe, Vincent entertained, he had let himself become deceived by humans once again. After all, their irrational senses, which they labeled in grandiose terms, were often a well-crafted means of justifying themselves

How could they be trusted? And what chance did he have pulling this off and getting these bands of rebels to actually make peace? The chances were slim to none. Even those within Acropolis and outlaying quadrants were blinded by their own narrow experiences of humans. How would he get them to make a truce?

The weight of it all was heavy to bear, but Vincent was aware suddenly of his own power too. He held the power to determine the fate of humans and humanoid-kind and influence the outcome of the war toward his own design. And, really, he entertained, who better than himself, someone who had experienced both sides of the war? The fibers in his neck tingled and he momentarily placed a hand there. Since he first existed, he had power only within the limits of his assigned job but now he was in a position of true power. He wasn't sure he wanted to take these humans the route John had proposed. Maybe there was a better route, he pondered. Maybe he should rule these humans and humanoids the way they should be ruled--a way made of his own design.

Vincent who had been looking down, deep in thought, lifted his head slightly to what came as a needed distraction to the dilemma. Way off in a far corner of the armory, he spied a tattered doll like the one he had seen in the war.

Or is it another illusion, Vincent speculated, *like the one I saw in the bathroom at the Inquisitor?*

He was reminded yet again of the sense of human need who, like this doll, were in some ways innocent (if not naive), exposed, and battered. He could see they were tired as they ran about making preparations, running on fumes of adrenaline and anxiety. He felt too the struggle within himself on what route he would take these last remaining humans. After a group of men congregated in his line of vision of the doll, and he contemplated human hunger of the soul, the men moved on but the doll was gone. He wondered if it had been there in the first place. It was then that he heard these words ring loudly within his being, nearly knocking him over:

"Vincent, lead my people."

Trial by Robot Companion

How the Companion is Broken Down

Group Discussion Questions: A moral and spiritual discussion focus

The Trial By Robot Multi-Verse: Describing symbolic references and allusions.

Questions for Group Discussion

1. Vincent represents another character in a popular sci-fi story from 1979 called "The Black Hole". In what ways is Vincent from "Trial by Robot" similar and different to the one portrayed in the classic film?

2. What is the significance of Vincent being aware of a tingling sensation around "fluid exchange fibers" in his neck? Why do you think he was trying to keep his neck problem a secret?

3. If you could change one thing about your appearance (as Vincent changed his nose), what would it be? Why? What do you think the change would give you? Better yet, is there anything the change may take away from you?

4. Vincent says early on "Human systems were remarkably complex but fragile," and "their egos and emotions over-ruled the better part of themselves, destroying everything good in their path." In what ways do ego and emotions get the better of you?

5. Some people try to numb their emotions in order not to face the reality of their circumstances or the past. How can emotions and allowing yourself to take the time to feel them help you in the healing in the process? Do you ever reason yourself out of "feeling" and thus healing? What does that look like? What is the ego? How does the ego play out in your life for good and/or bad?

6. Galatians is a somewhat popular book of the Apostle Paul's writing in Biblical text. Galatians 2:20 is probably the most quoted out of this book. Look up information about who the people of Galatians were. What was Paul saying in Galatians 2:20 do you think in light of this?

7. Vincent describes some of the humans he sees on trial as failing "to take their laws" learn the laws of their enemy. What are some challenges you face in which you could do better by learning how people operate and think the way they do? How could this help you to better work with them or around them?

8. In what ways is the character of John Woods like Jesus in how he acts and talks?

9. John Woods was considered despised and controversial not only for his spiritual like qualities that are highlighted in the story but also because of his hybrid nature. We too also struggle with various sides of ourselves we don't understand. What parts of you are in opposition with each other? What parts of you do you have difficulty accepting? What parts in others?

10. In today's society, no matter what culture you live in, there are groups of people who aren't accepted, are constantly put on trial either in literal courts or the courts of people's minds. What are some of those groups of people today? What lengths would you go in order to defend them? What lengths would go to for people who don't believe or practice the faith you do? What limits would be there?

11. What is the significance of the dirty doll that shows up in the story? Do you believe that Vincent really saw the doll again at the end or just envisioned it?

12. Birds are referenced in this story (in the center garden of the Supreme Chancery and John Woods mistakes the sound of his rescuers as a trapped a bird), what is the significance or symbolism of birds?

13. A picture of the fanatical religious leader "Nicodemus" shows him in priestly garb holding a cane with a curved hooked at the end. What could this potentially symbolize in religious terms?

14. Though Vincent agreed with his government that humans should be eliminated, why does he think John Woods should have had a fair trial?

15. Vincent, in his download, has a vision of a woman on trial holding a purse in front of her chest "protecting her heart". Who does this woman end up being and what Biblical character does she represent? What is the symbolic nature of her holding something to protect her heart as to the character she represents in the Bible?

16. Vincent refers to sensing Governor Wood's emotions at various points and grows more and more connected to him. Have you ever been aware of someone else's emotions but felt detached from them? How did that feel? What did you judge about yourself?

17. When Vincent is about to dive into the memories of the trial, he says "*This is it, the beginning of the end...*". Why do you think he said this? Have you

ever had a thought or vision that you didn't understand until later?

18. Cassandra and Dee-Dee are said to escort Governor Woods to the stand wearing high heels that "pounded the floor tiles with the fierceness of hammers pounding in nails" What is this in reference to in the Bible? How does this relate to what Governor Woods is about to go through?

19. In what ways are the list of charges that are read to John Woods by the court similar to those of the actions and character of Jesus in the Bible?

20. There are number of places in the trial that Governor Woods remains silent. Why do you think he chooses not to answer at all or until pressed to do so? What spiritual martyrs can you think of who lived the same way--stood silent before accusers. Why did they? What purpose does it serve?

21. Governor Woods is accused by General Iscariot of not being aggressive enough by not totally wiping out the humanoid army in the Valley of Ice when he had the chance to do so. Why do you think the Governor used restraint and did not wipe out the entire humanoid army? Do you think it was a wise choice?

22. Why do you think General Iscariot ultimately reveals a strategic plan of the Galatian Army operating through underground tunnels? Have you ever been so emotional that you said something you regretted? What did you do about it?

23. John Woods says that the humanoids may kill his body but that he will live on. What does he mean? How is this

similar to the message Jesus gave about his own purpose and power?

24. What is the significance of the Governor putting his betrayer, Petra, in his place of holding his mother Angela? What do you think about John Woods doing this act? Have you ever experienced that level of forgiveness where you were trusted again so fully after committing a terrible failure? Is it possible for humans to forgive at this level? Should we always show this kind of trust no matter what to anyone?

25. Vincent notes the elements of spirit and compassion as a form of almost transferable energy. Have you ever felt this? What examples do you know about of someone living a spiritual life that exemplified compassion that spread and healed others?

26. John says, "Mother, meet your son. He will take care of you now more than I ever could... Son, meet your mother. She has seen too much suffering. Give her safety and peace." Who does Jesus in the Bible give his mother to and why do both of "son"'s in both these stories choose to accept the role do you think?

27. One of the charges against Woods by his own people is that of him disappearing "in times of need". Are there any spiritual gurus of our history and times who did such things? Why do you think they did? Did they not care about those under their care.

28. What do you feel about the silence of God in your time of need? Have you learned anything from it?

Do you resent it? How do you handle this resentment?

29. When Chancellor Shackleton says, "Truth? What is Truth?", what Biblical conversation does this mimic? How is he like the Biblical Roman character who says these words?

30. Governor Woods uses this claim: "You may have my body, but you will never have me, for I am in this world but not of this world." This is a claim similar to that Jesus made. The word "world" in Biblical text doesn't mean our physical world but rather the world systems. In light of that context, What did Jesus mean by saying this and can we live it in today's world? Should we and at what level?

31. Is your faith more like a coping mechanism to get you through hard times or something "different" as Vincent observed in John Woods? What is the "difference" for you?

32. What is the significance of Nicodemus QT-1 being named after "Nicodemus" in the Bible? How was the Biblical Nicodemus similar to this one in "Trial by Robot"?

33. The white, thick book of the Descendants represents all holy texts being used in a way that is false. In what ways do people today often use holy books as the Descendants do, with falsehood and a lack of common sense?

34. Governor Woods calls the Descendants and Nicodemus "Blind Fools!" that are not only leading people astray but into grave danger. In what ways were the Descendants leading people astray? Are there groups or religious bodies that face the same

religious fanaticism today? Have you ever been deceived by religious fanaticism?

35. Petra is a betrayer reformed. In what ways is Petra like Peter in the Bible and spoken to like Peter in the Bible in this story? Why does Governor Woods call him the "one last hope"?

36. Think Star Wars and Darth Vader as reformed betrayer in the end. In what ways is Petra's story like the story line of Darth Vader in Star Wars?

37. What do you think of John Woods' rationale about the presence of a divine being like entering someone's kitchen or home when their physical bodies are not present? Have you ever felt God's presence in a significant way? Or any kind of supernatural presence? What did it do for you? How do you often miss seeing the miraculous, mysterious and supernatural in the everyday life? How could you change that and notice the unseen more?

38. Near the end of the story, the Governor commands Vincent to "Lead my people". This symbolic of the scene in the book of John 21 in the Bible. How is Vincent in a similar position as Peter in the Bible who these similar words were spoken to? Have you ever gotten a word from God or a sense of a mission that felt too big for you? What did you do? How do you encourage yourself and your faith so that you too can answer God's call when it comes?

39. Why do you think Vincent chose to disguise himself as the Governor when he went out to see the Galatians? Could this eventually backfire on him? What masks do you use to cover how you really

feel or who you really are? How is it working for you or not working for you? Could the masks backfire on you?

40. What do you think is happening when Vincent is struggling at the end of story to actually follow through with what John Woods commissioned him to do? How is this like us and the struggle we can have living out our own callings?

41. What is your prediction on what Vincent will choose to do after he hears that last phrase "Lead My People"?

42. What do you think was the significance of this story being separated into six sections in regards to the story of Genesis? In what way did humans betray God in the Bible? What was their relationship like afterward?

43. The Bible speaks of "Repairers of the breach: restorers of paths to dwell in" (Isaiah 58:12). By the end of the story, does it appear that Governor Woods wanted to build a bridge between humans and humanoids? How do you distinguish between building bridges with people and holding to set boundaries? How clear do you make this to others or do they have to figure it out? Is there someone in your life you wish you could meet in the middle and how might you edge closer to that? What would your life look like if that relationship was better?

Sci-Fi/Fantasy Layers

A. Character influences

Vincent--"The Black Hole" (see character section for more detail)

Ava--Hal, from "2001" (see character section for more detail)

Cassandra and Dee-Dee--Siren, from Tron Legacy

Nicodemus Q-T--Zues/Castor, from Tron Legacy

David--David Lindsey author of the book "Voyage to Arcturus"

B. Story Influences

I-Robot: Humanity being threatened by robots as well as saved by them. Also, the evolution of humanoid's "positronic brain" and the resulting "robopsychology" that developes because of the concerns. Asimov also develops these Three Laws of Robotics which actually influences some of the ethics of artificial intelligence today. Though these don't appear in the story, you will note Vincent's adherence to their "laws" which is inspired from I-Robot as well. The entire violation of laws that create a system of putting humans on trial is inspired by the story. Not only that, but also that the ancestors who were sympathetic to humans at one time making it so that the law that gives humans trials cannot be erased is meant to represent how the Three Laws cannot be broken either.

The Birthmark (Hawthorne): The inability of self and others to stand for anything less than a cultural idea of perfection.

Star Wars: The redemption of those on the "dark side" of the force. Also, the horror of those that are forced to become part robot, part human like Darth Vader was but on an even higher level, at the fetus level.

The Black Hole--A robot (in this case Vincent, a hybrid) saving humanity.

Star Trek (Dr. Spock)--Dr. Spock's struggle between his two sides of logic and human emotion.

Tron & Tron Legacy—technology taking over

Spiritual And Other Interesting Symbols

The Six Sections--Trail By Robot is broken into six sections. These are meant to reflect the 6 Days of Creation as depicted in the Bible. By the end of the story, a hybrid with a spiritual nature and the mission to heal his world is created.

The year 2888--the number 8 is a lucky number, it also has Biblical significance. (There are 3 eights in 2888 and 3 significant set of eights in the Bible; the eight sons of Abraham, the eight writers of the Gospel, the eight times Jesus showed himself after his crucifixion.)

Vincents tingling neck fibers--represents his human side that is unwilling to be silenced. This sensation keeps Vincent grounded to his body.

"Galatia"-A name chosen for two symbolic purposes. On a simple level, it is a place that is under Arctic conditions and the name is a play on the word Glacial. On a deeper level, it refers to the book of Galatians, one of my favorite books and often quoted book of the Apostle Paul's writings.

The Betrayal of John Woods--this is done in a form similar to that of Jesus Christ by his own "tribe". Jesus's own fellow Israelites handed him over to the Roman Government, the very rulers that persecuted them.

Room 71a--this is the room Vincent is assigned to in the Grand Inquisitor hotel. It is a flip of my birthday, the 7th day of January (1st month). The small a, is for my middle name Andrew.

3 Days of Trial--This refers the three days Jesus was in the Tomb.

Numbers within Court Documents

1. Chip specs---15.5 (John 15:5) 4.10 (I John 4:40) 2-4r (Romans 2:4)
2. Model #'s of the humanoids on the Tribunal--all are considered unlucky numbers
3. Composition Square, Room 121 is reflecting the book of Romans 1:21
4. Quadrant 316 reflects the popular verse often quoted in the Bible John 3:16

Ava--She is very loosely meant to be modeled after 2001's HAL with her Big Brother like traits. Like Hal, we can only hear her, not see her. She too ultimately betrays Vincent as Hal also betrays the humans.

Governor Woods hair--His bangs are said to go to the right. Jesus is said to sit at the right hand of God.

Governor Woods silence--Jesus is often portrayed in silence before accusers.

Shackleton's address on the word "Truth"--This is similar to a conversation that is said to have taken place between Pontius Pilate and Jesus where the Roman Governor asks Jesus the same question: "What is Truth?".

John Woods saying "my life and truth speaks for itself" -- many spiritual gurus and martyers often point to how they live their lives and not just their words as an example for people to follow. Yet how many quote the words of Mohammed and Jesus like models to beat others down as well as use the words out of context as a weapon.

The relationship between Petra and Angela--John Woods is our Jesus like character. He is very forgiving and appeals to Petra simply through the power of his eyes and presence. Much like in the Jesus story when Jesus is about to die on the cross, Jesus introduces the Apostle John to Mary as "man meet your mother" and to Mary as "mother meet your son" in light of his upcoming absence from this world. This Biblical development in the Jesus story, shows how strong the love is in the bond between mother and son, for even Jesus on the cross bothered to assign to these characters to each other, in the midst of great suffering. John Woods models Jesus in re-introducing these two characters to each other as mother and son, but he goes further in this story. The betrayed Governor puts his trust in someone who had just betrayed him. This goes the extra mile. John Woods gives Petra the high responsibility of taking care of his mother.

Birds--Birds and Angels share the symbolism of spiritual growth and guardians in literature. Even though the Supreme Chancery is one of the most powerful institutions in Acropolis, birds still have infiltrated its center garden area. Evil cannot keep out the light. Also, later in the story, John Woods mistakes the sound of a rescuer as the sound of a bird pecking at something, trapped in the room next door. This ends up being his rescuers.

The Envoy's dress heels in the courtroom--the envoys, Cassandra and Dee-Dee, usher John Woods to the stand and their heals are said to sound like the pounding of nails. This is meant to symbolize to the crucifixion of Jesus, being nailed to the cross.

Governor Woods' Blind Fools Speech to Nicodemus--This is mimicking the speech Jesus gave to the Pharisees in his anger about how they were the blind leading the blind. Nicodemus represents a futuristic group of fanatical zealots.

"Lead my People"--John Woods gives Vincent his exaltation which is what Jesus said to the Apostle John before departing to the heavens; "lead my people" and "feed my sheep".

The damaged pull-string doll--she stands as symbol of the vulnerability and neediness of the human race and a haunting reminder for Vincent of the cruelty exacted on humans by his own kind. Whether Vincent was really seeing the doll again at the end of the story, reminding him of human need or not is up to reader interpretation.

"The Descendants of Hewlett Packard"--This is meant to be a bit comical and shows how all of us can be blind when we get fanatical and think we have a corner on the truth. The "manual" and his attachment to it is meant to represent many today who worship books like the Bible and lose human compassion quite willingly..

Character Names

"Vincent: Model G220": Vincent is the name of a robot in the Sci-Fi story "The Black Hole" who becomes an unwitting partner in helping the crew of the spacecraft USS *Palomino* escape. In our story here, Vincent tries to save humans as well. Vincent's model # G220 refers to a popular and one of my favorite scripture verses, Galations 2:20 "I have been crucified with Christ and I no longer live, but Christ lives in me. The life I now live in the body, I live by faith in the Son of God, who loved me and gave himself for me." By the end of the story, Vincent is trying to live out this very verse.

"John Woods": John is his first name because my favorite Gospel is the book of John and Woods refers to his famous quote of Jesus referring to himself as the Vine, and we the people as the branches--all items contained in the "woods" or earth. Jesus is both of the heavens and of the earth.

"Chancellor Shackelton": Clearly, his last name refers to the word "shackels" in that he imprisons but he is also imprisoned by his own sense of superiority.

"Petra": Petra represents the Apostle Peter. He is introduced first as the lead betrayer of the Christ-like character, John Woods. Peter is said to betray Jesus three times in the Bible. Petra turns out to be Governor Woods rescuer and he is told that he will be the "key to the kingdom" of what remains of the human race. In a similar sense, Jesus tells the Apostle Peter that he is leaving him the keys to the Kingdom and he would be the foundation, the building blocks, of the church despite his betrayal.

"Angela Woods": Angela represents the mother of John Woods and is symbolically representing Mary from the Bible who also witnesses her son Jesus on the Cross betrayed and suffering. "Angela" is a play on the word "angel". She is also given over to Petra as his "mother" in much the same manner Jesus gives the Biblical Mary over to John as his mother when he is dying.

"Mary Woods": Mary is John Wood's wife and her name is a play on the idea that some suggest Jesus had more than friendly ties with Mary Magdalene. Some believe they were married or perhaps some kind of love interest.

Sergeant Isador and Asg: These two names came out of robot name generator online just for the fun of it! In essence, a computer helped me generate names for walking computers. Ha!

General Iscariot: Judas Iscariot is the name of the Apostle that betrayed Jesus as the General does in his testimony against John Woods. He also reveals, in his anger against John, a major military stronghold and plan of attack during his testimony. In movies, Judas is portrayed as wimpy man but here I wanted to portray him in the opposite because the Bible really doesn't give us any idea about him except his betrayal.

General Quinn: Francis Quinn is a character in Issac Asmov's I-Robot who was cunning. It is also a name I meant to sound similar to Flynn. This is the last name of Sam Flynn in the movie franchise Tron and Tron Legacy who fought against an army of electronic warriors and machines.

"Nicodemus, Model QT-1": Nicodemus' model # "QT-1" refers to the name of a robot in Issac Asimov's stories I-Robot. In addition, Nicodemus is the name of a Pharisee in the story of Jesus the Christ who can't quite get his mind around the Christ and pleads to reason from him. The Pharisees were a very religious sect that ended up turning the Christ over to the political power of Rome. The character of Nicodemus' persona is somewhat modeled after Michael Sheen's portrayal of Zuse/Castor in Tron Legacy who runs the End of the Line club.

"Cassandra" and "Dee-Dee"--Although there is nothing symbolic in their names, the personas of these characters are meant to be reminiscent of the two Siren characters in Tron Legacy that dress Sam Flynn before his battle debut.

"David": Represents the author David Lindsay and his book "Voyage to Arcturus". The main character Maskull starts his journey climbing a lot of steps and goes to Arcturus struggling with issues of life and death. Here in our story, this "David" is climbing around in the vent shafts and facing the struggle of life and death under the threat of being caught. He eventually chooses to save himself.

About the Author

LA Jamison

LA Jamison is Author and Owner of Got Words? Publishing (www.gotwords.org).

LA conducts activism through his writing as well as expresses his creativity through his blog, movie and book reviews at Got Words? He has two prior works self-published and another full-length novel on the way. He has a Bachelors of Science in English Education and Communications/Theater Arts for Teaching and works with the special needs children population. He has been an active volunteer in his community wherever he has lived. He resides presently in Detroit, Michigan and can be reached at lajamison@gotwords.org,

LA_Jamison on Twitter and LA Jamison on Facebook.